AF819645

A Black Christmas

Brothers Black Series Bonus Book 8

Blue Saffire

Perceptive Illusions Publishing, Inc.
BAYSHORE, NEW YORK

Blue Saffire/Perceptive Illusions Publishing, Inc.
PO BOX 5253
Bayshore, New York 11706
www.BlueSaffire.com

Ordering Information:
Quantity sales. Special discounts are available on quantity purchases by corporations, associations, and others. For details, contact the "Special Sales Department" at the address above.

Cover Designed by Covers by Combs

A Black Christmas/ Blue Saffire. -- 1st ed.
ISBN 978-1-941924-12-9

What is love if it's not shared with someone who sees your soul?

—Blue Saffire

PREFACE

Dad

Joe

"You're here early," I say as I walk in to find Roni in the basement gym at the office.

She sits on the edge of the ring, taping her hands. When she lifts her head, I note the hesitation in her eyes. My sons have all picked lasses who are perfect for them. However, John couldn't have picked more perfectly for himself.

"I knew you would be the only one here," she says.

"Which means you're looking for me. Here, let me help you with that," I say as I sit next to her and reach for her hand to tape it. "What can I do for you, and how much trouble am I going to get into for it?"

I bump her shoulder as I tease, bringing a smile to her face. I know a secret. Roni is a big softy. She loves hard and is dangerously protective, but once she cares, she cares. She's a lot like my boys. Fiercely possessive of her own, she's just not going to show it.

She looks down at her hand I've finished taping before shyly looking back at me. Her cheeks glow with a blush. Very out of character for her, which gets my attention.

"You know the wedding is coming..." She takes a pause and sucks in a breath before releasing it heavily. "I don't have a dad to dance with me. Cass said if... if I wanted, I should ask you."

The big tears that fill her eyes tug at my heart. I wrap an arm around her shoulders and kiss the top of her head. It takes me a moment to clear my throat.

"I'd be honored, Roni. If you want me to walk you down the aisle too, I'm here. No need to ask, I'll be there," I reply.

She pulls away and gives me a wobbly smile. "You would do that?"

I return her smile. "Without question, love. In fact, how about we make this our practice time for our dance. I already have an idea."

Her smile grows and lights her entire pretty face. I see why John is so smitten with her. Roni is a lovely young woman inside and out. When she allows you to know her, she makes you want to protect her and show her love. Like a kitten that's been tortured and now only wants affection.

"Okay. Cool. It has to mean something though. I don't want to dance to any meaningless sappy shit."

I wink at her. "Never even crossed my mind."

CHAPTER ONE

My Wedding

Joe

Three months later…

"You did good, son," I murmur to myself as I look at the smile on John's face as he looks down at Roni in his arms.

Now this is some wedding. John made sure Roni had the day of her dreams. Snowfall indoors, ice sculptures of the two of them as well as one with Mena in John's arm as Roni stands tucked under the other. The detailing is out of this world.

They've captured my little granddaughter and her cute dimples in all their glory. They even caught the intensity in Roni's eyes. I've never seen such realistic sculptures.

Crystal lighting and flowers hang from everywhere. Blue and white roses fill the room. I don't think Ireland has ever seen a sight like this. Although John would only allow Cass and I to pay for half, it was well worth every penny to see the smile on Roni's face.

We've grown closer in the last few months. I consider all the girls to be like daughters, but Roni has become my buddy. I took great pride in walking her down the aisle to my son earlier.

Looking around at my boys, I smile. We did good. Cass and I can sleep well at night knowing we raised real men.

"What are ye thinking?" Cass asks as she walks up beside me.

"They're all men now. Despite all of their shenanigans and hardheaded decisions." I scoff and shake my head. "I never thought I'd see the day they were all married with children."

"Aye, I never thought we'd have grands. The little whores were taking forever to fall in love. The lads gave us a run for our money, they did. I can't wait to see their wee ones give them all their shit back."

I laugh from my belly. She's right, they took after me. I found my way into quite a few knickers in my day.

Cass wraps her arms around my waist. I place my hand on her hip and look down at her. I'm glad I decided to claim this fiery woman. We've lived a good life and still have more years in us.

"Aye, I'm with you there. The boys are already taking Noah to task. Jordan will be a hand full if you ask me."

"That little one is a troublemaker, but I'm wrapped around her tiny finger," Cass says lovingly.

I sigh. "One more wedding to go. I think I'll be sad to see the end," I muse.

Cass groans. "I think I'm going to kill him before the damn day arrives."

"Oh no. Speaking of the devil, here he comes." I chuckle.

Ryan comes storming our way, looking like a disheveled mess. He wipes the sweat from his forehead with the heel of his palm. Placing his hands on his hips, he then blows out a breath.

"How am I supposed to top this? What the hell? I didn't know he was bringing in ice sculptures.

"Did you know about this? He made her a fucking winter wonderland in the middle of Ireland. Do you see the look on Carmen's face? God, I hate John's ass," he rambles as he pouts like the big baby he is.

Cass sighs and rolls her eyes. She turns from me, moves closer to the lad, and crooks a finger at him so he bends to her height. When Ryan gets eye level with her, she pinches his lips between her fingers and twists.

"Now ye listen here," she starts. "Ye won't be making me crazy with this. Ye hear me? She's going to be surprised and it will all work out if ye calm yer arse down. Enough."

She releases Ryan with a shove and moves back into my side. I wrap my arm around her again as I watch our son and the sullen look on his face. He pushes a hand through his hair and frowns.

"I'm fucking this up. I know I am," he grumbles.

"This might be true. You've fired four wedding planners, changed the location three times, and you freak out every time Carmen looks at you too long," I say between my laughter.

"I want it to be perfect. I shouldn't have rushed her to go to the justice of the peace. First Felix's wedding, now John's. She looks like her heart is breaking," he says.

"And all ye have to do is make it to Christmas. Or have ye changed the date again?" Cass replies, her words dipping in sarcasm.

"What? You don't think I should have picked Christmas?" Ry's eyes look like they're about to come out of his head.

"For fuck's sake. He's yer boy, ye deal with him," Cass says and walks off.

I move to place a hand on Ry's shoulder. "Listen to me, lad. You need to relax. In a few months, it will be over, and you can breathe."

"Yeah, okay, but you're sure you can get the cherry blossom trees for me, right?"

"Ry, get out of my face," I grunt.

I've told him a million times Kiyoshi and I have taken care of those damn trees. We've tracked down someone to genetically engineer the damn things out of season. He will have his trees.

Cass is right. I'm going to wring his neck before he gets to the altar. Right as I get ready to shove him in the furthest direction from me, John walks up and tugs Ry into a headlock.

A huge grin on his face, John messes Ry's hair before kissing his head and letting him go. Ryan grumbles while fixing his hair and tugging at his tux jacket. My heart swells. I can see the love they have for each other, even as Ryan mutters to himself.

"Don't worry, little brother. You're going to pull this off," John says.

I snort. We all know how much Ryan has been stressing. I warned him from the beginning. Carmen wanted a wedding of her own, not a courthouse visit.

He was so shaken by almost losing her, he wasn't willing to wait long to make her his wife. He's always been the impatient one as the youngest. Cass is a saint for dealing with him.

"Did you really have to show me up like this? How much was that damn necklace you gifted her this morning?" Ryan huffs.

"Why? So, you can get Carmen a more expensive one?"

"Duh, asshat. She's mentioned it at least a dozen times."

"Bite me, dipshit."

Ryan inhales, then his face lights up. He snaps his fingers. "Fuck that. I'm knocking her up. She loves being a mom. I'll give her another baby."

"Ryan," I warn.

"I got this, Dad."

"Just let it go, Dad. He's special. Nothing we can do now," John ribs.

I roll my eyes and let Ryan disappear. Apparently to make me another grandchild. No doubt he'll manage to make that happen. Ryan can do anything when he sets his mind to it.

"You ready to tell me what you and Roni have been up to?" John says, pulling my attention back to him.

I chuckle. John has been wondering what Roni and I have been doing since our first meeting. Every morning she has dropped the babe off with Cass and made her way into the office early.

I pat him on the shoulder. "You'll find out soon enough." Roni appears as if on cue. She gives me a nervous smile.

"Ready?"

I wink at her. "If you are."

"Yeah, as I'll ever be," she says, peeking at John out of the corner of her eye.

John raises his brows. Suddenly, his face softens with understanding and he turns to look up at me. He tugs me into a tight hug.

"Thanks, Dad. This means so much to her and me," he whispers.

"Wait until we're done before you thank me." I give him a good squeeze before releasing him and holding out my arm to Roni.

"Here goes nothing," she mutters, taking ahold of my forearm.

John

"Where are you going?" Wyatt says as he comes out of nowhere and holds me back by my shoulder. "Stay right here."

The smile on my face grows as my curiosity gets the better of me. I fold my arms over my chest. I haven't been able to wipe this smile off my face all day.

This is Roni's dream wedding. Under it all, my wife is a girly girl. This wedding couldn't be more of a contradiction to what she shows the world. I don't mind.

Anything she wanted, I made sure it happened. She deserves it. We've had a rough few years. It feels good to finally be able to breathe and be able to focus on planning and having a wedding.

I hate we had to wait so long, so there was nothing Roni could have asked for that I wouldn't have made happen. She could have asked for the moon in her palms at the crack of dawn and it would have been hers.

Mom appears at my side and places a hand on my back. "He's been excited for this moment. I've caught him shaking his hips around the house," she says as she smiles at my father and wife.

My wife. That shit feels so good to say. I plan to own that ass tonight while she screams *my husband* the entire time.

"I can hear yer thoughts, my kinky fucker. Thank goodness I'm keeping my little Mena for the week. I'll keep ye from corrupting her for as long as I can," Mom says.

I turn to look down at her with a cheeky grin before I lean in to whisper. "You do know I found Dad's stash. The tapes, whips, cuffs, and some other shit I had to learn to understand years later. That's where I got my start."

Her face turns bright red. "Ye tell a fib."

I wink. "Not at all."

"Ye do know I'll still kick yer arse," she hisses back at me.

I throw my head back and laugh. My laughter is cut short as the music catches my attention. My gaze falls on Dad and Roni as Bryan Adams croons "Everything I do."

Tilting my head to the side, I draw my brows in. Roni looks gorgeous. The crystals all over the bust of her gown cast a glow against her skin. I've been admiring that effect all day.

The Cinderella skirts—as Roni called them—were the right choice. Everything about the dress compliments her. She looks like a true doll.

I can't help wondering why this song. It's not exactly a father-daughter type of tune. That's when the lyrics begin to replay the part when he says it's worth dying for. The words echo in the air and then the melody from Prince's "I Would Die 4 U" starts to play.

Dad and Roni push away from each other and start to roll their shoulders and arms, mirroring Prince's dance from *Purple Rain*. I start to laugh.

Like *Grease*, this happens to be another of Roni's favorite movies, and its Dad's all-time favorite. When the hook starts, they point to each other and break into the whole signing of *I will die for you*. That shit hits me in the heart. I know Roni and

Dad have gotten close, but this shows how close. Roni does nothing she doesn't mean.

They continue to dance, but as the hook comes back in, they turn to face me and Mom. I take note Wyatt has moved off to the side a bit. This time when they sign, *I will die for you*, Roni points to me as Dad points to Mom.

I'm so filled with emotions. I know she would. We've been there and came too close.

At the bridge, Roni lifts her skirts as she and Dad do some fancy footwork then start a grapevine to the right and return left. The intensity in Roni's eyes as they sign the hook once again tells me all the things I know.

Mom leans into my side as she sways to the music. I glance at Dad's face for a moment. It's clear he's sending Mom a message too.

One I've always known, but it's so much more powerful in this moment. I wrap my arm around Mom and we both sway as she moves her arms around my waist.

That's when Val and Tasha run up behind Roni and release the skirts from her dress, revealing the crystal covered part of the dress is more like a corseted bodysuit. I grind my teeth, not too happy about this.

Daddy and Roni turn and shake their butts like Prince. Mom starts to roar with laughter beside me. I'm still not that amused.

"He still has a fine ass," Mom chortles.

The song changes and curiosity wins out. Busta Rhymes "Touch It" starts to play and I get the outfit. Roni and Dad are about to show out.

"Okay," I say and nod.

So, if you don't know, my dad loves to dance. My brothers and I can dance, but Joe Black can dance, dance. This is the perfect song for him to show off to.

I know my competitive ass wife. These two are about to have some fun. And that is what makes me relax and enjoy the show.

They stand side by side. Hands turn out like Egyptians as they rock and bob their heads. The motion grows bigger as they bend their knees and rock from side to side, still bobbing their heads with the movement. As the beat drops, they start a body roll and pump their arms in front of them.

"Get it, Joe," someone calls out.

The room goes wild. When the beat slows, they get low and start to bounce as they move to face each other. Damn, Dad's still got it.

Dad gets low, elbows out as his fists touch and he bounces his shoulders left to right. Roni claps it out for him as he gets into his own groove. Then it's Roni's turn.

The smile on her face has my chest so tight. God, I love her. It took so long for her to show her joy openly like this.

"They'd both do anything to see you happy," Mom says.

"Yeah, I see that," I choke out.

Roni and Dad turn the moves into a little Samba like dance and I have to say I'm impressed. That's when Mom pulls from my side and starts to do a little dance toward them. I purse my lips. Mom will never have a rhythmic bone in her body.

Suddenly, I notice almost all the women I know have my wife's back move toward her and Dad. This time when Dad and Roni get low, Roni is the only one who reappears as all of the women surround them.

They start to clap on beat and Dad raises slow. When he fully stands, he looks around and pops his collar. Roni throws her head back and laughs. She then holds out her arms and starts to shimmy her body to the beat.

All of the women reform and get behind her, but that's not what stands out. It's the hiss and breathe noise that comes from them that gets my attention. It sounds like a hiss followed by the word "life." It cracks through the room like a whip.

Roni jerks her body every time they say it. Soon she's facing me, and the women are all lined up behind her. Each one holding the waist of the woman before them. Val is the one right behind Roni.

Warriors.

That's what I know they are. All of them. Roni, Val, Tasha, Paige, Pam, Nellie, Bean, Kamara, Kaye, Carmen the list goes on and on. They will die for Roni and their families, and she them.

I'm so captivated by them. I hadn't noticed Wyatt and Noah appear at my sides until they start to make an answering sound to the women. The sound thunders through the room and that's when I look behind me. My other brothers, my cousins, uncles, and friends are all lined up behind me like the women are behind Roni.

Felix steps up behind me and pounds his chest as all the guys let out a collective "*Whooo*" in response to the ladies' hiss. I turn to face Roni again and her eyes are on me. I nod my head at my wife, I get it.

I loosen my tie and shrug off my jacket to toss it aside. Felix places his hands on my waist and plants his head in my back. Wyatt and Noah place a hand on each of my shoulders. Wyatt stands on my right, Noah on my left.

And we move. We dance our way toward my wife, and she marches toward me. So much emotion fills Roni's face. Tears fill her eyes.

When her knees buckle, I know it's not a part of the routine. Val catches her under the arms and locks her hands over Roni's shoulders. They pause and Roni sways a bit to the music.

Nellie and Bean pop out and grasp her biceps. Roni looks up through her lashes at me. I wink and crook my finger at her. She nods and gets back into her groove, all while the women behind and beside her support.

"Yes, Lord," Pastor Porter croons.

Roni starts to pump her fist and gives herself over to the music. A roar rips from her lips, and I feel that shit in my soul. We've fought hard to be here and here we stand. I take note of my dad and mom out of the corner of my eye standing on the right outside of the center where Roni and I will meet.

"Black," Wyatt and Noah boom beside me.

"For life," the women respond.

"Black," all the guys repeat this time.

"For life," the women reply louder. Roni is the leader with a huge smile on her face.

When we meet, I place my forehead to hers as everyone continues to chant around us. Mom and Dad come to our sides. Dad places a hand on each of our heads and mom places a hand on my back. I believe she has the other on Roni's.

The moment is so powerful. I'm choked up. I'm reminded of the day we did this for Wyatt and Nellie.

It's a reminder they always have us, and us them. All of them. I grab Roni's hands and lift her arms over her head as we roll our bodies together. Pinning her with my stare, I warn her not to drop them as I skim my fingers back down her body.

"Black," I whisper to her as I cup her full ass and pull her into me.

"For life," she says with tears in her eyes.

CHAPTER TWO

Joe Has Moves

Roni

I've never been this happy in my life. I look over to my daughter in Cassie's lap as I dance with my sexy husband. LaSalle walks over and lifts Mena into his arms. He tickles her and she begins to laugh.

When LaSalle turns to me, he finds my eyes on him and sends me a wink as he lifts Mena's arm for her to wave at me as he says something to her. Her big eyes light up and she starts to clap.

My face heats as John grinds his hips behind me. I'm not sure how I feel about grinding my ass on him as our daughter watches. I start to question my parenting for the hundredth time.

John snakes his arm around me and cups my throat, bringing my back to his chest. "Stop thinking so much. She will see you show affection her entire life. She will also see me cherish you and place the world at your feet. She will know what love looks like and how to make the right choices," he breathes into my ear.

"You think you know me so well," I reply.

"I do." He kisses my forehead.

I smile. I've been doing a lot of that today. The song changes to Beenie Man's "Wickedest Slam" and a holler goes up. I turn to the right and find Joe grinding on Paloma Nash and Mrs. Porter behind him grinding her booty on him.

Joe has one hand on Paloma's waist with his tongue hanging out of his mouth. Sweats drips from his face as he wines his hips. Brooklyn strolls over and starts to roll his body as he stands in front of Mrs. Porter. He's not half bad. That New York swag drips off of him.

"I love your family," I say without thinking.

"Our family," John says into my hair.

"Our family."

I close my eyes and take in the moment. My body hums from John's nearness. I can't wait until this is all over. The craving I have for my husband threatens to consume me.

"You haven't been off your feet in hours," he says as the song comes to an end and the DJ changes to some old smooth R&B.

My feet are starting to hurt, but I wouldn't dare tell him I want to stop dancing with him. As long as I'm in his arms, I'm happy. I don't get to tell him this.

John wraps an arm around my waist and leads me over to the tables that have been pushed together by a few of the guys. Cassie has Mena once again as Cassie sits with her brothers and smiles. However, this time Cass is in Joe's lap and my daughter is in her Grandma's lap.

I go to take Mena, but Cass frowns at me. "Leave her be. Enjoy your day, love."

John tugs me into his lap and locks his arms around me. Placing a kiss in the crook of my neck, he gives me a gentle squeeze. I settle in and look around the tables.

I take in the O'Briens and McGowans. Man, it's like everyone's family has expanded. It's funny to see how they all come together for these moments. There are sure to be laughs all around this table.

I shift my gaze and find Paloma Matsumara-Nash now sitting in her husband's lap with a smile on her face. Mrs. Porter sits beside Pastor Porter as he has an arm around her shoulders. Then there are my brothers-in-law and their wives.

I catch Carmen with that inquisitive look on her face as she looks between Cass and Joe and her own parents. I can see she's looking for the story, but she's too shy to ask. I'm used to that now.

Deciding to help her out, I turn to Joe. "John told me you two met at a party or something. You met dancing, but how did you end up together?" I ask.

"Wait, you two met at a party?" Nellie says.

"Aye, we did," Joe says with a smile. "One look and I forgot all my problems and why I was there in the first place."

"I knew she was gone when she didn't signal for me to come clobber him. I may be the youngest, but I still looked out for my sister," Uncle Ronan says.

"Ye were too busy with your nose in that's lass's neck. Besides, ye sent the brute to chase after me. I was set up. You weren't going to help me."

Ronan laughs and winks at his sister. He shrugs. "Aye, she had no idea he was in Ireland for her." He lifts his hand in surrender. "Besides, I had nothing to do with that, but you're right, he was the first lad I saw tame ye. I had nothing to say."

"Wait, you're forty-five, right?" I ask Ronan. He would have been too young to be at a party with Cass back then.

He frowns. "Don't ye listen to my sister. She tells people I'm five years younger than I am to get away with lying about her own age."

Cass looks around the room and whistles. Ronan laughs and takes a drink. "I'm only five years younger than she is. I was a big lad for fifteen when they met. I would go to parties with her to clobber anyone who got out of line, no one knew I was so much younger."

"He looked old enough to be twenty," Cass says with an affectionate smile.

Carmen places her elbows on the table and her head in her palms. I almost giggle at the sigh she makes as she sits in anticipation of the story to come. I'll admit I'm right there with her.

"I've heard everyone else's story. I would love to learn yours," Carmen says.

"Maybe we should put the wee ones to sleep first," Cass says, with a wicked grin. "Pastor ye, may want to exit too."

"Gal please, go on. You think me and my wife don't know how to be naughty. Please, you forget we had two pickney of our own."

"Suit yerself."

CHAPTER THREE

Dancing Fire

Joe

"Brick House" by The Commodores blares through the speakers of this house party. The host is American from what I understand. I don't mind as I rock my hips, while trying to land my lay for the night.

I look out of the corner of my eye at Eric, one of my friends. We've served together for four years. This is the most uncomfortable our relationship has ever been. Others warned me, dating his sister was a bad idea.

However, those long brown legs and hot pants got the best of my common sense. One shake of those tits in my face and I was all hers. The breakup wasn't even my fault. She cheated on me. Claiming she was lonely while I was away on tour.

I can't blame her. What was supposed to be six months turned into a year. Sasha is young and stunning. She's full of life, I'm sure guys have been banging down her dorm room door.

I certainly spent my fair share of time banging at it. We've parted as friends. However, her brother doesn't seem to want to let it go. His sister had some fun with an older guy. She got to brag to her friends about sleeping with a military guy. All things she sees as a win, her words not mine.

"This feels awkward, man," I say to my old buddy.

I'm trying to chat up a pretty blonde, but he keeps glaring at me. If I didn't possibly need him for this mission here in Ireland, I wouldn't have asked him along. It feels good to be able to kick back and I want to enjoy it.

A good shag would be icing on the cake, but I can't make that happen with one of my best friends glaring at me. I'm six five to his five ten. Trust me, he knows this is a fight he's not ready for.

Eric shakes his head. "Listen, man, I don't see how you can move on so easily. You were just with my sister selling her dreams. It's like your white ass couldn't wait to use those moves my sister taught you on some white bread chick."

"I sold ye sister nothing. We're friends and we intend to stay that way," I say through clenched teeth.

"Friends don't fuck," he snaps. "I heard you two before we left to come here."

"Aye, she wanted to say her goodbyes. We're not mad at each other."

"So why do you sound so mad? Your accent is slipping."

I thin my lips. I guess he's sort of pissing me off. Sasha had cornered me and asked could we have one last good fuck. Of course, I said yes. She does this thing with her ass when she's riding me, I wanted the experience one more time. However, I'm not going to tell him that.

"Fuck you, Black," Eric says, but the heat in his words has gone.

"No, I want to fuck *her*," I say, pointing to the lass in front of me.

She stares back at me with a deep red blush. She's pretty, I'm going to enjoy this. Right as I get ready to lean in and seal the deal. The song changes to "You Dropped a Bomb On Me" by The Gap Band and something on the dance floor catches my attention.

It's the red hair that draws me in. The lass can't dance to save her life, but her arse is cute in her bellbottoms. She turns and her face comes into view. I indeed feel like a bomb has been dropped on me. Where the lass I'd been chatting up is pretty, this tiny no rhythm having thing on the dance floor is stunning.

The tops she has on wraps her full breasts and bares her midriff. Her pale skin glitters under the lights. The black fabric of her clothing is a stark contrast to her fair skin and fiery red hair.

Her red locks are cut into thick bangs as the rest feathers around her face. Giving me a Farrah Fawcett vibe. She has a cute nose and gorgeous lips. I'm too far away to see the color of her eyes, but those hips. Those hips she's flailing about are calling my name. I think the thing to get my feet moving in her direction is when I note how small she is.

I tower over her as I stand behind her. I snort as she wiggles around looking as if she's having a seizure. I reach for her waist and pull her back into me. Splaying my hand against her front I start to move our bodies together to the actual beat. It takes a second to get her on task with me, but soon, I'm rolling my hips into her plush little arse.

When she looks up at me, the air is knocked from my lungs. She's even more breathtaking up close. Her eyes are a pretty hazel.

Cassie

I widen my eyes as I look up at the giant standing over me. The first thing to pop out at me are his golden eyes. His dark hair and long lashes make his eyes startling against his tanned skin. His height is next.

The lad is handsome, and he can move. And fuck me, his pecker is stabbing right into my bum. It's a big one for sure. I wrinkle my brows, wondering where he came from. I made a turn about this party and didn't see anyone nearly as handsome as him.

He flexes his fingers on my waist still grinding against me. Suddenly, I turn and grab him by his balls.

"Ach, do ya make it a habit to go around pawing on lasses ya don't know?" I hiss, trying to keep from my face how impressed I am by the handful of cock in my palm.

He grabs my wrist and spins me, wrapping his hand around my throat and pulling me into his chest. The scent of his cologne engulfs me. My nipples pebble against the thin fabric of my halter top. He dips his head close to my ear.

"If ye are going to grab it. The least you can do is tell me yer name."

"Augh, yer American," I huff. Although his words are wrapped in a Scottish brogue, I can tell he has an American accent as well.

"I'm Scottish born, Love. Moved to the States as a young lad."

"And that be too American for me. Release me before I break yer knee caps."

He chuckles as if I've told a joke. I grew up with four brothers. I don't make idle threats. Speaking of brothers. Where the heck is that damn Ronan? I didn't sneak his little arse in here to be abandoned.

"Yer name, Lass. I want to know the first name of the future Mrs. Black."

I snort. "I assume ya to be Mr. Black?" I scoff. "Think highly of yerself, ya do. My Da can't marry me off to a wealthy Irishman, what makes ya think I'll give ya the time of day?"

"Yer body for one. I bet if I stuck my hand in yer knickers, they'd be soaked for me. Look at how your nipples are straining for my attention," he breathes against my neck, causing a shiver to slide down my back.

"Ya be a cocky fucker. I hate arseholes who think too much of themselves."

"But I promise you, I'll back every single word up, love."

His words bring on another shiver. I pull free of his hold and walk away from the hottest dance I've ever had and the sexiest man I've ever met.

CHAPTER FOUR

Business Stop

Joe

Eric had a good laugh over the little redhead who blew me off. I, on the other hand, haven't been able to stop thinking about her. I force my thoughts of her to the back of my mind for this mission.

It's not an assignment from my SEAL team. It's a favor my da has asked of me and my skills. I'm still not clear as to what I'm doing here. It's why I brought Eric along in case.

All I do know is I'm meeting with the eldest brother of the McGowan Clan. I've known Jonah for some time. I can't imagine what they would need with me. The McGowan name comes with its own reputation.

As I turn onto their property, I'm reminded of Scotland and my own family's homeland. Rolling hills, acres of green lands.

It's been so long since I've been back home. Not since my sister's wedding and the birth of her oldest son. She's pregnant again so I'll be headed home soon. Although, my father has mentioned a time or two her husband plans to move them back to Ireland where he's from. Our relationship with the O'Brien clan is strained at best, not so much with my brother-in-law, but his father is another story.

Mick's da doesn't much like Scots. I had to make sure he understood he'd treat my sister with nothing but respect no matter his feelings. O'Brien has a lot of shit with him.

"Well, I'll be," Eric mutters beside me as I drive up the driveway to the large house.

That's when I see her. The redhaired lass from last night. She's in a pair of high waisted short shorts and a thin strapped T-shirt. Once again, no undergarments in sight. Her nipples are in plain sight. Her milky white skin is a bit flush from the hot sun. Those red locks bounce as she walks with a basket of what looks like herbs on her hip.

It instantly clicks in my mind she's a McGowan. She has the same red hair. She's only missing the blue in her hazel eyes I know her brothers for. I can see it now.

The nose and the heart-shaped lips. I think she's more stunning in the light of day. I grow aroused from watching her thighs turn red from rubbing together.

Images of her little ass turning red under my palm fill my head. I plan to spank her for last night. I shift in my seat from the memory of her grabbing me with her small palm.

I want her to grab me again, but in a more familiar way. Hopefully while on her knees as I take ahold of that hair. Those lips wrapped around me as I plug that feisty mouth of hers. Let me see her sass me after I have her submit to me.

"Joe, look out," Eric calls out.

I slam my foot on the breaks and turn away from the little spitfire who has bewitched me. A cow stands before my truck. I almost slammed right into it. *Shit.*

"Damn, man. She really did a number on you," Eric says.

I'm starting to wish I'd asked Rob or Chase to do me this favor. If they hadn't had plans I would have. The cow moves as I grumble for Eric to shut up.

I focus on the road and make my way to the house. In the back of my mind, I can't help wondering who this lass is to Jonah.

"Joe," Jonah croons as he steps from the house. "Good to see you, Black. Ronan tells me ya ran into our sister last night."

"I might have."

Jonah laughs heartly. "I hear she had ya by the balls. I fear ya may have a challenge on yer hands with this favor we need to ask of ya."

I draw my brows as curiosity fills me. What exactly has my da gotten me into? Jonah pats me on the back. "Come on inside. We need to talk."

Just then the little fireball walks by and up to the front door. She looks at me with wide eyes before she schools her features and heads inside. Her plump little arse in her tiny, tight shorts grabs my attention. All thoughts of never dating one of my friend's sisters ever again, goes out the window.

I lick my lips. As if knowing I'm staring, she turns and looks over her shoulder. She gives me a cheeky grin, looking down at her arse then back up at me. She winks, before dropping all warmth from her expression to scowl at me.

"Jonah, why is he here?"

"Da wants to speak with him," he replies.

"About what? It better not be about what I think it's about."

"Ya would rather our family have to go to war then do what Da asks you to?"

"I don't see ya going off to marry a lass with the bake of a cobbler's thumb."

"And this one? What's the problem with him?"

I stifle the choke that tries to rise from my throat. My father didn't tell me this mission had anything to do with marriage. Although, I wouldn't mind being a husband to this lass.

Cassie

"So ya knew who I was last night?" I say to the golden eyed giant.

"Not a clue, love."

I huff. I take him in. He's more handsome than he was last night. The fabric of his tan bellbottoms hugs his legs and that impressive package I held last night. His white shirt sits open as the top buttons are loose. His muscles stretching the sleeves of the shirt. No, he's not the 300-pound bloke my father had initially tried to marry me off to, but he's still not *my* choice.

I want to fall in love. I don't want to be a bargaining chip for power. I want to be able to choose for meself.

"Don't you live in the states?"

"Aye, lass, I do. When I'm not deployed."

I growl. "So, Da wants me to move to the States and leave my family behind. This is too much."

I put down the basket of herbs I've been carrying to Ma, who's most likely in the kitchen. I glare at Jonah and this stranger.

"Ya can go fuck yerselves. I won't take part in this, I won't."

I am so furious at this point. Not one of my brothers were forced into an arranged marriage and here my father is trying to force me to either marry into a mob family or to some stranger who lives in America. I've never left Ireland. I don't know the first thing about America or this man.

Apparently, I started some trouble when I told that fat fucker I would marry him over my dead body. Now my father has been scrambling to find me a suitable match who can stand up to the Kasey family. If I don't find the right husband who can protect me from my own mouth, then my whole family could be in ruin. All because I refused to marry that slob and didn't bite my tongue about saying so.

Honestly, the pig actually had food in the corner of his mouth. The sight of him made my stomach turn, there was no way I would marry such a creature. He looked at me like I was a slab of meat. Not that this one hasn't looked at me as if he's ready to gobble me whole.

He says he didn't know who I was last night, but he had to in order to be so bold to put his hands on me while me brother was in the same building. And didn't he say something about me being the future Mrs. Black? How did he not know who I was? Now here he stands today. Looking delicious and completely edible.

I want to run my hands through that dark hair and nibble on his plump lower lip. Lord that's a lot of lad to climb. I've never been afraid of a challenge. The question is, is he really sure he wants to take me on?

"*Deirfiúr*, he didn't know who you were. Joe doesn't even know why we called him here."

"Don't sister me."

Jonah sighs. "Da hasn't had a chance to talk with him. Ya might have just scared him away," Jonah says.

"A wee tantrum isn't going to send me running for the hills. I intend to hear ye father out. I'm intrigued. I'm not sure why I'm here, but I believe I might be willing to help ye out once I understand everything that's going on.

"*I believe I might be willing to help ye out once I understand what's going on*," I mock.

"Your Scottish accent is pretty good," he taunts.

"It's better than yours, you American," I sling at him.

He gives me a smug grin. Rolling his eyes over me as I stand with my hands on my hips. My chest heaves with my anger. I feel like I've been set up. My choice is being taken from me.

"Fine, take him to Da, but good luck with getting me to agree with the marriage." I snort and stomp off to my room.

CHAPTER FIVE

A Match

Joe

Cianán McGowan sits behind his desk as I enter the old study with Jonah. Jonah moves to the small bar and starts to pour drinks. I take the seat in front of Cianán's desk.

I left Eric to wait out in the drawing room. Something tells me I no longer need his help. If this is about what I'm thinking it's about, I definitely can send him back home.

"Welcome, Joseph. Thank ya for coming to see me."

Jonah places a glass in front of me and then moves to hand his father the other one before leaning to whisper something in his ear. My interest is piqued as a grim look comes over Cianán's face.

"I'm sure yer wondering why you're here."

"Aye, I am."

"Jonah tells me ya met me daughter twice. I gather ya understand she's a bit spirited."

I chuckle at that understatement. That lass is a tornado of fire. I would love to tame that fire in my bed.

However, marriage at twenty-five. I'm not sure if I'm ready to concede to the idea. Sure, my father has rambled about me settling down with a nice lass. However, I've been busy with my military career. Homing my skills and figuring out a way to maximize them once I retire.

I'm guessing Da decided to go ahead and make the decision for me. Wouldn't be the first time he stepped into my life like this. Moving to the states wasn't my choice. Neither was joining the service. It was all what Da thought was best.

"Here's my dilemma, Joe. The lass doesn't realize how deeply she offended the Kasey family. Her words and actions have stirred up quite a bit of trouble. Now I have to find her a match the Kaseys wouldn't dare challenge and who can keep her safe.

"Yer Da and I have been friends for years. And when it comes to the Black clan. I know the name strikes its own fear. A match between the Blacks and the McGowans would be just what I need to keep the Kaseys at Bay.

"Not that I think they can handle us if they try to bring this war. The problem is we have too many mutual friends and business ventures. It's bad for business. We stand to lose too much. Now the question is… is your Da right? Would you be willing to take the lass on?"

"First, I'd want to formally meet her. Then I'd like to ask her a few questions I have for my future bride. Then I'll make a decision and let ye know," I reply.

Cianán laughs. "I'm almost tempted to force ya to answer now before ya meet her. She's a good lass, she just has a bit of a temper."

I shrugged my shoulders. "There's nothing wrong with that. As long as her temper is directed in the right direction."

"Unfortunately, I'm quite sure it's directed in yer direction," Jonah says.

"Och, I believe that to be so. I've handled worse and survived." I clap my hands together and stand. "All right, I haven't spent a night in my home in a year. Let's get on with this."

It's the truth it's been a year since I stepped foot in my L.A. apartment for longer than thirty minutes. I would love to have the comfort of my own home and shower. I've been thinking more and more about settling down. To have a place where I can lay roots after each tour.

To have a wife of my own, waiting there when I return, has an appeal to it. Especially after the debacle with Sasha. I'll admit even though I wasn't angry, I was a bit hurt. Just a wee bit.

We'd talked about marriage a time or two. However, I knew she was still young and not ready to settle down. I wonder if this lass is also a bit too spirited to handle my long tours away.

"By the way, what's her name?"

"Cassidy, we all call her Cass or Cassie."

I play her name over in my head. *Cassidy.* It suits the wee lass. I can't say it's going to be a hardship getting to know her. Pretty face, pretty name, and a body to fill my dreams while I'm away from home. The Black men are faithful to a fault.

Sure, I had women throwing themselves at me when I was overseas, but I never cheated on Sasha. Cassie wouldn't have to worry about that either. Ronan comes rushing into the room as we start for the door.

"Joe, you're still here?" he says with a confused expression.

"Aye."

"Then why is Cass leaving?"

"What?" Cianán roars.

I just saw her tossing things in the boot of her car. From the looks of it she might be headed to her cabin.

"No, the lass isn't that daft. A rainstorm is coming in. It's sure to wash the road out. She'll be trapped and vulnerable," Cianán groans. "I had three lads, why didn't I stop there?"

"We have to go get her before the Kaseys find out she's up there alone or worse. She trapped in." The thought of being trapped in with the wee terror causes me to open my mouth with an offer.

"I'll go. Just tell me where to find her."

"She'll blow ya head clean off yer shoulders, she will," Ronan warns.

"Aye, the lass keeps two shot guns up there," Cianán says.

"Ach, Kasey and his boys are in for a bit of a surprise if they intend to ambush our sister." Jonah snickers.

"Aye, but I still don't want to leave it to chance. I think the lad should go. Ya need to be careful when ya approach. She's a grand shot."

"We'll see about that. Do you mind giving my friend a ride to the hotel? He may want to return home."

"He's welcome to stay here and get langered with us. We'll show him a grand Irish time," Jonah croons.

I look between Ronan and Jonah. I can already see the mischief in their eyes. Ronan pushes his red hair off his face, and

I get the feeling the wee redhead got her feistiness from the men in this very room.

Not a single one of them truly begrudges her for who she is. It may actually be the other way around. They respect her for it.

Cassie

I'm not the one to sit around while others decide me fate. I packed me things and took off for the cabin grandda gave me, so I'd have somewhere to get away from all of me brothers when they start to do my head in.

I drop back onto the King-sized bed and blow out a breath. Running a hand through my hair, I try to settle my thoughts and anger. Da doesn't listen to me. I'm only some silly girl he needs to clean up after. I resent the way he treats me.

The entire family coddles me and then gets upset when they think I'm being a brat. The brat they created. Well, they want a brat. Here I am.

My mind turns to a certain pair of golden eyes. His dark lashes complement them so well. I've never seen a man with such pretty eyes. How can I forget the way he moved his hips on the dance floor?

What did Jonah say his name is? *Joe.* It suits the big lad. And big he is. *Gah, what's wrong with ya Cass?*

My cheeks are flushed, and my nipples have tightened from just the thought of him. The way he moves that big body with such ease and power. Phew, I could use one quick shag in his bed.

Not too quick. I want to savor running my hands through his dark hair and over his broad muscle. All while that sexy voice rumbles in my ear. I gave him shit for his accent, but I like it.

It's American with a hint of Scottish as if he could never forget home. I can't help wondering if I too will be able to keep my accent if I move to the States.

Move to the States for what?

I calm my wayward thoughts. No one's going anywhere. At least, I'm not. I leap off the bed to find something to eat. This is my cabin, but my brothers often use it to bring their trollops here to shag.

They tend to eat up all my food and never remember to replace it. Once in the kitchen, I growl as I see they've done it again. My cupboards are bare.

Suddenly, rain starts to pound the roof. I tighten my hold on the refrigerator door handle. My anger rising.

"For fuck's sake, why is it so hard to stock my food back up. Bunch of slackers."

The rain starts to come down harder. It dawns on me I could end up stuck here foodless and frustrated. I want to scream. The sound of tires rolling over grovel catches my ear.

I rush to the door and pull my shotguns. If Kasey and his goons followed me here, I'm going to send them all back home blown to pieces.

I step back from the door with my guns aimed. A large frame stops before the door. I can see their outline through the glass and curtain that hangs over it.

"Cassie, this is Joe. Don't shoot, love. I've got food for ye. Looks like ye'll need it. I think the road has already started to wash out and yer brother said he left the place bare."

That voice. It hits me in the core. I have to swallow hard as I think of my next move. I can't speak for fear, I'll give away my true reaction to him.

"Cassie, I can see ye shadow, love. Can I come in?"

I clear my throat. "At your own risk."

The door creaks as he slowly pushes his way in. He effortlessly balances bags of groceries in his hands. I swallow hard again when he has to dip his head to come inside. He turns to close the door behind him. My face heats and I raise a brow as I get my first glimpse of his tight arse.

He turns busting me the same as I had him earlier. His soft looking lips turn up in the corners and he gives me a cocky grin. I've yet to put me guns down, so I cock them at my sides and cross my arms back over each other.

"Why are ya here?"

He rolls his eyes. "I can leave and take this food with me. Ye can starve, ye wee bandit."

My face burns with anger. One of my brothers could have easily made the trip to bring me supplies. I allow my gaze to follow him to the kitchen as realization hits. I've been set up.

"Ya best be leaving before ya can't get back."

He swings his gaze to me. "Ye know yer not safe here alone. Ye have people after ye."

"What's it to ya?"

He looks pointedly at my shotguns. "Clearly, you're no damsel in distress. I'm here as a friend."

"A friend of who?"

"Jonah, but it could be to you. Why not get to know me, before you decide to shoot me?"

"We don't have time for that. Do ya hear the rain? We don't have long before yer stuck here. There's only one bedroom and if trees fall with the flooding it could take weeks not days to get back."

He shrugs his big shoulders. His eyes heating as he stares at me. I bite my lip. *Yeah, I wouldn't mind being trapped with ya either, big lad.*

I shake my thoughts away. I need him gone before I do something stupid. I'm clearly very attracted to him. I've wondered what it would be like to live in the States a number of times since he walked through that door.

The distinct sound of a tree snapping pulls my attention. I lower my guns and rush to the window. I groan when I see one of the largest trees on the property has fallen behind his truck.

He's officially trapped in. Neither of our cars can get around that tree. I turn to look at him. "Looks like ya just became me roommate."

He roams his gaze over me. "Not complaining, Cass. Not complaining at all. Why don't you come help me put these things away? Then we can get to know each other."

"Fine," I grumble.

CHAPTER SIX

What We Can Be

Cassie

The giant keeps surprising me. He has cooked a romantic dinner, finding candles in one of the cupboards as he went to set the table. I'm trying not to be attracted to him, but I'm failing.

He's gorgeous, he can cook, and his voice is like an enchanted spell. I wish I had on a thicker top or at least a bra. My body has been giving me away.

From my protruding nipples to the blush taking over my entire body, I've exposed myself, and from the grin on his wicked lips, he knows this.

"Would you like to take dessert into the living area? You can tell me why you're so against what your Da wants."

I nod my head unable to find words. Which is so unlike me. I honestly don't know why I'm fighting my Da so hard anymore. Not when this is my newest option. The truth is, I would have said yes on that dance floor if Ronan had told me who he was.

I help to clear the table. As I place the dishes in the sink, our arms brush. I feel like I've been zapped by electricity.

I jerk my arm away and look up at him. His eyes have darkened as they meet my gaze. I place a hand on his bicep, causing him to turn into me.

I step into him and run both my hands up his arms to his chest. He wraps his strong arms around my waist.

"I have a question for ya. Why are ya so okay with this? Has my Da offered you a handsome dowry?" I wrinkle my brows. "We're not paupers, but I can't see him offering enough to make ya want to do this."

"Yer selling yerself short, love. I've been offered no dowry. I have two eyes of my own. We certainly have the chemistry."

"We know nothing about each other," I whisper as I look away from those intense eyes.

He cups the back of my neck and bends toward me. Like a magnet pulls me, I lift on my toes and met him halfway. I've never been stupid a day in my life until today.

My stomach drops and my toes curl in my runners. Sparks explode between us. I moan into his mouth, surprising myself. He growls and deepens the kiss, his hand on my neck tightens.

When he pulls away, he winks at me. "It looks like we've already started to get to know each other. How about this? We forget about your Da and what he's asking of us, and we just get to know each other. If you don't like what you learn, when they come to get us out of here, we go our separate ways."

I nod and smile up at him. Knowing I'm probably not going to get a better match, but also liking the idea of having a choice.

So far, he's shown himself to be sweet and intelligent. He also has a sense of humor, which a man needs to have to deal with me.

He takes my hand in his. "Come, let's sit."

We move to the old brown sofa. My belly is full, and I have this sense of comfort around this relative stranger. At least if I have to be saddled with this one, I don't have to worry about looking at him. He'll make a handsome brood. I can see them now. My red hair and his gold eyes.

Stop it Cass. We don't want a husband. Not him, not anyone. Ya're only twenty. Ya have a life to live.

"How old are ya?" I blurt out.

"Twenty-five, and ye?"

"Twenty."

Joe

I can't help staring at her mouth as she says her age. I want to taste her again. Her mouth had been salty and sweet from the steak and potatoes I made for us. I enjoyed watching her savor the meal. The lass isn't shy to enjoy a meal. I like that.

When she asked why I'm so willing to consider this arrangement, I had to ask myself the same thing. I'll be straight with myself.

I was a bit wounded by Sasha and her actions. She admitted herself she had regretted the choice and in the end, it was lackluster in comparison to me. I think I see Cass as a challenge. Eventually, she has to choose me. My ego needs her to make that choice.

And once she chooses, she will be my wife, which means she has to be faithful. At least that's my fucked-up logic at the moment. Although, I'm smart enough to know none of that means she has to remain faithful to me.

I'll make her a good husband. I'll be faithful, I'll protect her and provide for her and the children I want to bury inside her. Those hips were made to carry my seed. She may be tiny in height, but that body packs a punch.

"Are ye in university?"

"I've taken a few classes, but I'm needed to help at home, so I'm taking a break."

"Why don't you want to marry?"

Her eyes light up and she surprises me when she spins in her seat and topples back onto my lap, throwing her arms over her head as she sighs.

"I want to see the world. I want to live life, not have life live me. I want to go with the wind. Ya know what I mean? I want to see the world, I do."

I love her Irish lilt and the nuance of her speech. It's so Northern Irish and it encourages my accent that my time in the States and in service has tried to erase.

"Aye, I get ye, love."

She reaches up to cup my face. "But ya would leave me stuck home in… where do you live?"

"L.A. at the moment. I used to live in New York for a bit."

"Ya wouldn't leave me in L.A. never to travel and learn new things, would ya?"

"No, love. Tell me where ye want to go and I'll always make it happen. I want our children to be cultured and to speak as many languages as I do if not more."

She pops up off my lap with those words. I gather she's not interested in having bairns. A shame because I've already been imaging our wee 'uns bouncing around this cabin during summer visits. Fiery red hair, her hazel eyes and that cute nose.

Disappointment fills me. I hadn't realized I wanted a family so much. The wee lass brings all types of feelings to the surface. I say my Da knew exactly what he was doing.

"What's on ye mind?" I ask.

She shivers. "This conversation feels too real."

"Maybe that's because it all can be." I give her a warm smile. "Do you want children?"

"Aye, I do. I always thought I'd marry an Irishman. Not a Scott. Especially not one from America. No offense."

I snort. "What do ye have against Americans?"

"Nothing. It's not them it's what happens to you when you go there. You've been washed away. Your accent is softer. I can tell. When was the last time you ran through a prairie? Do you remember what a Scottish winter feels like? I want my children to know these things."

"And they will. If we were to marry, we'd spend summers in Scotland or here with our bairns. We'd come for holidays. I've never missed a Christmas with my family. Not unless I'm on assignment."

"How often is that?" she asks and drops her eyes to her lap where she's playing with her fingers.

"I plan to put in a few more years before I retire. My friend and I want to start a business first to have something to fall back on. Between his connections and my resources, ye will never have anything to worry about. We could have ten bairns and travel the world," I reply. "Do you think ye could handle that? A few more years of my serving?"

She licks her lips and her brows pinch. "I don't know. I'll be alone. I don't know anyone in L.A. and ya would be gone."

I slide a little closer to her. Closing the gap between us. I've been dying to kiss her again.

I slip my hand into her hair and tip her head back. "I promise. I'll make it all worth it," I say against her lips.

She whimpers. I take it as an invitation to crush my lips to hers. I tug her hair harder, testing to see if I can push her limits. Her moans increase and she locks her fingers in my hair.

I smile into the kiss. It may be buried deep, but she has a submissive in there. I'd love to pull her out. Sasha had a ton of hard limits. I respected them, but it put a lot of restraint on me. I'd love to see how far Cass would allow me to go.

"Cass, think about it. We could be great. I'd spank ye for touching what's mine after every tour. Ye could sit on my face for the first twenty-four hours, so I could remind ye who owns this pussy. I'd worship ye like a queen, love."

CHAPTER SEVEN

Yes, Please

Cassie

What did he just say? I didn't think it was possible for him to get any sexier. I bite my lip and look up into his eyes. I'm throbbing between my legs.

My defiance wains. My da knew what he was doing sending this man after me. *You don't want to marry the slob with stains on his face and shirt. Here's a sex god. Now what Cass? Tell me no now.*

"Ah, fuck, come and kiss me," I huff.

He chuckles but sits back against the sofa as I climb into his lap and cup his face between my hands. His dark silky hair feels so good between my fingertips. I want to ride his big arse like a champ.

Not that I have a clue how. That's how insane he makes me. I want things I know nothing about.

He palms my arse, and all bets are off. I'm like a pressure cooker. My lid is ready to blow. He kisses me hungrily. I give back just as good.

I don't realize I'm grinding in his lap until he squeezes my arse tightly, holding me still. He swats my left cheek. I pull away and look at him through wide eyes. It stings, but I'd be lying if I didn't admit my knickers are wet.

"I'm saving myself for my husband," I blurt out.

"Good, so we can fuck until we have to go, because I'll be your husband before the year is out."

I scoff. "I'll have me brothers lay boots to ya, if ya don't make good on that promise."

"Och, I never make a promise I can't keep."

The glint in his eyes tells me this is true. I reach for the hem of my tank and pull it up over my head. He hisses out a breath and squeezes my cheeks once again. His eyes have turned so dark they're almost a deep honey brown.

I cup my breasts and lift them in offering. Joe wastes no time dipping his head and receiving. He wraps his warm mouth around one peak while thumbing the other with one of his strong hands.

I throw my head back and start to rock in his lap again. His thick, long length grows beneath me. I'm eager to unwrap him and see it for myself. Joe has the looks to rival a movie star.

I release my hold on his hair to grab for his muscles. They flex under my palms. I suck in a breath and moan.

"I want you so bad," he groans against my breast.

"Please," I pant.

"Beg some more. I love it," he says huskily.

"Please, I need ya."

"Aye, love. That's it. I'm going to make sure ye remember me."

Tilting me back so his hand behind my neck is my only support, he then claws his fingers down my belly to the waistband of my shorts, causing me to shiver.

Swiftly he moves us, so I land on my back on the sofa with a small bounce. He presses into me with his weight. It's a heady feeling. I reach to run my hands up and down his back.

I want to feel his skin against mine. I reach between us for the buttons of his shirt. My fingers tremble as I release the tiny closures.

However, his hot breath against my neck is comforting. He seems to become impatient. Gently, he takes my hands and lifts to sit back on his heels. Releasing my hands, he then begins to unbutton the shirt on his own. I marvel at the tanned skin that comes into view.

He has a washboard stomach and broad chest. Everything I know about sex comes from me brothers and their naughty films. While his chest is impressive, I want to see what's beneath his bellbottoms.

Seeming to read my mind. He reaches for his belt and tugs it loose and off. I reach for his zip, I haven't gotten it down, but he's already straining against it and the fabric. I pull it down slowly as not to hurt him. I don't realize I'm holding my breath until he springs free.

He pops out looking heavy and then pops back against his taut belly. No undies in sight. My mouth waters.

"Eyes up here, love."

He reaches beneath my chin and lifts my head. My gaze snaps to his.

"Save that hunger for later. It's my turn to feast." He makes quick work of removing my shorts. I almost feel shy as my bare arse is revealed along with the red bush between my thighs.

However, the moment desire and lust fills his face I grow bold. The thought of this big lad losing his control over me, brims me over with pride and joy.

He leans in to kiss me again. It makes me feel silly with joy. I gasp when he starts to hump his hips against me and his length slides back and forth across my folds. I pray for him to slip inside where I need him most. My essence gushes forth, preparing me for him.

He reaches between our bodies and rubs my magic bundle of nerves. I begin to rock my hips, greedy for more. I whimper in disappointment when he removes his hand. Yet, the disappoint doesn't last long as he lowers onto his belly and hooks me legs over his shoulders.

I yelp and twist away when he begins to suck on me lower lips. My stomach caves and my legs quiver. I reach for his hair and tug. It's too much, yet not enough.

"Joe," I scream and what feels like a thunder bolt hits me. My entire body convulses as my vagina feels like it has a heartbeat of its own.

He looks up at me with a cheeky grin and sucks on my pussy lips once more for good measure. He lets them slip out of his mouth slowly. Right when I think he's done. He scoops his hands under my arse and lifts it up in the air so he can feast some more.

This time it's even more intense. I try my best to ride his face and ride the wave of pleasure he's sending through my body.

"Yes, Joe, yes. Christ."

He hums like Winnie the Pooh with a pot of honey and keeps slurping through my cries of ecstasy. Those golden eyes focus on me and my head scrambles.

For a moment, I stop to think about what this all will mean, but as if sensing my thoughts, he sucks my attention right back to him. I run my hands over his big arms he has wrapped tightly around me.

Suddenly, he backs off and lowers me. While on his knees, he palms his shaft and starts to stroke it. A look crosses his face, but he shakes away whatever the thought is.

He bites his lip and lowers to hover above me. I wrap my legs around his thick body. Breathtakingly slow, he enters me. Oh God, this was a mistake.

Joe

I bite back a growl as I enter her tight sheath. She's so slick for me, but she's still a tight fit. I groan loudly as I fully seat myself. Once again, I'm hit by her father's words before I left.

Give the lass a babe. I'll send her to ya within three months. I can hold things off that long at least. She'll be grateful to me in the end.

I take pause to think of using a condom, but I want this. I want her. If in three months she shows up on my doorstep to tell me she's carrying my bairn, I won't be upset in the least. I feel a deeper connection with her in the last few hours than I've felt with anyone in years.

I groan as I move in and out of her slick walls. They're squeezing me so tight. She writhes her small body beneath me.

Each time she calls my name it's like she's wrapping around my heart like a siren's call.

Reaching for her left leg I hold it against my side as I thrust deeply into her. The deeper I thrust, the deeper I want to go. I'm holding back just a bit, not sure if she can fully take me.

"I can handle it, Joe. Stop holding back," she cries out.

With those words, I allow my inner beast to release. I take her lips and kiss her savagely, while plowing deeply into her. She throws her head back against the cushions of the sofa and starts to thrash her head back and forth.

"Oh my God," she cries out.

She's so wet the sound starts to echo through the room. I lift her leg to my shoulder and start to nibble at her ankle. Lifting her arse from the sofa, I rock, grind, and swivel my hips. Pinning her legs back into her chest with a firm grip on the backs of her thighs, I then look into her eyes and continue to thrust.

Her chest and breasts have flush with her pleasure. As she calls out my name and other things that aren't making sense. I pull out and turn her over, placing her on all fours. Swiftly, I thrust back into her wet heat. Her wetness inviting me in easily. My cock is coated with her essence.

I throw my head back and roll my eyes into the back of my head. She feels so good. Her heat swallows me like a warm mouth. While watching her round bum bounce against me, I slap a hand across one cheek.

She cries out in pleasure, so I do it again and admire the pink hue that appears across her flesh. I palm her breast and guide her to bounce on my length.

"That's it, love. Take what you need," I dip my head to say into her ear.

She starts to make a keening sound. I know she's close, even though I'm nowhere near ready. I take her mouth in a deep kiss and savor the taste of her, banding my arm across her breasts as she convulses against me.

What has to be two hours later, we're both covered in a thick sheen of sweat. She's straddled across my lap as one of her breasts is in my mouth. I let it pop free from my lips when I feel the waterfall of her orgasm drip down my balls and into the crack of my ass. It's like a trigger for my own orgasm. I release deep inside of her, gripping her hips tightly. Still thrusting a few more times.

I cradle her against my chest as she quakes and quivers. Softly, I kiss her temple. She has a sleepy grin on her face as she looks up at me.

"Ya might just make a grand husband," she says, sounding punch drunk.

"Aye, ye will make a grand wife."

I nuzzle her neck and close my eyes. Images of small lads with my eyes dance in my mind. I may not agree with this plan of her da's, but I'm certainly looking forward to the outcome.

CHAPTER EIGHT

My World

Joe

"Tell me what your life is like?" Cass says as I run my fingers across her thigh.

She's lying against the head of the bed with one leg bent. I'm lying in the opposite direction, allowing my gaze to lazily appraise her body and face.

We moved into the bedroom after a shower. I would have liked to place her in a bath to soak, but there isn't one here. Instead, I've oiled every inch of her body after our shower. Relaxing her muscles and worshiping her skin.

"I have an apartment I share with my roommate, Eric. I've been thinking of moving into a house soon. I just haven't been home long enough to make it happen. I'm on assignment a lot as the commander for a special ops team.

"I have a sister. She lives in Scotland, but I think she's moving to Ireland soon. I have a huge family. My father is the oldest, so he oversees most of the family."

"Oversees?"

"Yeah, my father runs the family businesses. The Blacks have a lot of connections and far reach. Dad keeps it all going."

"How did you get to New York?"

"I moved to New York with my uncle when I was around ten. I'd lost my mum and Da was a bit lost himself."

"Oh, no. I'm so sorry. How'd she die?"

"She was murdered. I remember my father being so angry. I never knew by who, but I believe my father does."

"Sounds like he was protecting you."

"If you know my father, you know he's planning his next move, like the great chess player he is. I know what he needs me to know, when he needs me to know it."

"But you truly had no idea why he sent you here?"

"I can't say I'm surprised he sent me here."

I sit up and lean in to kiss her lips. I'm not surprised, but I'm becoming grateful. The more time I spend with Cass the more I'm endeared to her.

I turn to lie down beside her. Reaching over, I brush my hand over the ticklish part of her side. Her laugh and smile are infectious, and she has such a wondrous view on life. She's everything I loved about Sasha and more.

"Ya have to take me to New York, I want to see the Statue of Liberty and go to all the shops," she says with a dreamy look in her eyes.

"Love, there are so many places to shop in New York, you're going to have to be a little more specific."

"I want to see them all."

I laugh, but I know I will take her as soon as I get a chance. Not able to keep my hands to myself, I run the backs of my fingertips over her breast, bringing her peak to a pucker.

"I think you should make a list."

"A list?"

"Aye, I need to know all the places I'll be taking my wife."

She blushes and turns away from me. Her stomach rambles. "Ya can start by taking me to the kitchen for now. Did I see ice cream in those bags?"

"Ye did. I can make a sundae out of you," I say and wiggle my brows.

"Listen, you giant Scot. I need food. I can't eat cock for breakfast."

"But you can eat ice cream for breakfast?" I lift a brow.

She shrugs. "It's edible and I'm craving it. Cock is not a food and I can't eat it for breakfast."

"Aye, love, you can. Cock does the body good."

She lifts and straddles my hips. Her breasts jiggle in my face. I'm enjoying this lazy morning. I could wake to her and that smile every morning.

She leans in until we are nose to nose. "The sooner ya feed me belly, the sooner ya can feed me your cock." She kisses my lips. "Any. Place. Ya. Want. To. Feed. It." She punctuates each word with a kiss.

"A lass after my own heart." I chuckle.

CHAPTER NINE

Falling Slowly

Cassie

I keep telling myself not to allow my heart to run away from me. However, I've fallen for this giant in what has only been three days. When he's not making my body sing for him, he makes my heart stutter as he makes me laugh and smile.

That handsome smile of his is a weapon. He hasn't shied away from using it either. We've created our own little bubble here.

"What's on ye mind, love?"

"I'm trying to see our lives together beyond this."

"Any luck?"

"A bit." I smile.

"Do you like what you see?"

"I do. I didn't think I would, but I do."

"Good, we can go tell yer father, I'll be taking you off his hands."

A smile spreads across my face. I look at him dreamily. I think I'll have a good life. He has catered to my needs each day and has been interested in my every word. Even when I forget myself and my words run together from speaking so quickly, he makes the effort to follow me.

"Come, let's go for a walk. We can get some fresh air."

"Did ya clothes dry?"

I washed his things for him last night. I'm hoping we can get out of here soon. My Da and brothers know we're here, they should come to check on me soon. They will find the blocked road and cut us out. We have enough food to last us a few more days if needed.

"Aye. I believe they are."

He gets up and goes to get dressed. I get up and pull on a sundress and sandals. He appears in the doorway when he's dressed, looking as sexy as the day he arrived at my front door.

Soon we're off walking the small path to the lake on the property. I look up at Joe as we stop by a big tree. He leans against the trunk and pulls me into him.

"Your hair looks like golden fire in the sun," he says and brushes a hand across my cheek.

"Your eyes are more intense like this," I say.

He places his hand behind my neck and leans in to kiss me. He deepens the kiss as I moan into his mouth. I wrap my arms around his neck and allow him to lift me and turn my back against the tree.

"Joe," I whimper as he presses me into the tree and kisses his way down my neck.

I wrap my legs around him and cradle him between my thighs. We fumble with his pants to get them down his hips. I cry out and look up at the sky as he pushes into me and takes me against the tree.

He kisses me breathless, and I know in this moment, I'm so far gone for Joe Black. I'm falling slowly and I don't want this to stop.

CHAPTER NINE

Different

Cassie

I wake in the king-sized bed and stretch my sore body. Places I never even imagined feeling sore with a sweet pain. My mum would probably lay boots to me for what I've allowed this man to do to me every day and night since we've been here.

It would be worth it. I've enjoyed every second of it. I open my eyes to find golden ones looking back at me. He strokes my cheek and plants a kiss on my lips. I can't help smiling at him.

However, it doesn't take long for me to realize something is different. The smile is gone from his eyes. I get this feeling of impending doom.

I sit up quickly, holding the sheet against my breasts. If he thinks he's about to use me and leave me he has another thing coming. I meant what I said about my brothers kicking his arse if he slept with me only to try to throw me away.

He made a promise and I intend for him to keep it. I've never been foolish about men, and I don't plan on being foolish now. I'll shoot him with one of those shotguns before he tries to leave me here, without making good on his word.

"They've been cutting at that tree all morning. I think we're almost in the clear to go," he says, bringing my attention to the sound of the chainsaws outside.

"So, we're going to tell Da that I'll be leaving with you? We can return in the spring for the wedding?"

"Aye, love. That sounds grand but you won't be leaving with me. We can wed this spring when I return. They've been trying to reach me. I've gotten a comm for an assignment. I'm being deployed."

"What?"

"Don't worry, I'll talk to your da. Everything will be set up and you will have time to think about whether this is really what *ye* want. I want it to be your choice. I don't want it to be forced on ye."

My temper flares and I jump from the bed, pulling the sheet around me. I don't know what kind of games he's playing but when I offered him my body that was my way of saying I agreed to this, there's no turning back. All or nothing.

"You know what, Joe? You can get out. Don't worry about telling my da anything. I'll find my way. There has to be something I can do to fix this mess I've made without having to chase after or follow behind ya. Get out."

I have no idea why I'm so hurt. Just four days ago I didn't even want to get married. Now I feel like something has been snatched from me. My heart aches and my cheeks burn with embarrassment.

He holds up his hands. "Wait, yer getting upset for no reason. I thought I would have more time, but I have to report in."

"I bet ya just couldn't wait for a call like that to come in so ya could free yourself."

"Love, I couldn't have known this would happen. I honestly intended to take you back to America with me and get you settled. Please just give me a chance to make this right."

"You can make it right by getting out. I don't need a husband. I can leave and begin to travel and the Kaseys will never find me."

"But yer family will still be here. It will still be a problem for them. Don't be rash, love. Allow me to do what I need to do to ensure yer safety. Don't let that hot temper be the ruin of your family."

"Ya don't know what yer talking about. This won't be the ruin of anything. If they come for my family, we'll destroy them. I won't be forced into a loveless marriage. Ya don't even know me. Get out."

"Cass," he growls.

I stomp my foot, then storm into the next room to get one of my guns. He's hot on my heels, fully dressed mind you. I spin on him with my shotgun in hand.

"I said out," I snarl.

He runs a hand through his hair and heads for the door. My chin trembles as I fight back tears. I wait until he walks out to collapse to my knees and sob.

I tighten the sheet around me, then fall onto my side and curl into a ball as I sob.

Stupid, stupid, girl. Why would he stay? He got the cow and the milk for free.

CHAPTER NINE

Missing You

Joe

It's been four and a half months. I've called her every day when I could find time. Cass hangs up on me every single time. I've had her brothers deliver flowers for me. I've even sent jewelry.

They tell me she's thrown it all away. If only she understood how much I miss her. I was devastated when Eric brought my bag with the radio that had been going off while I was out of touch. I'd planned to make love to her all morning, then make her breakfast. Before settling to talk more about our future.

I never wanted to force her to leave with me. I wanted to make sure she left when she was ready. Always her choice.

However, she read right through me, and I did what I will always do with Cass, I told the truth. Her and those shotguns. I still have the image of her holding tightly to her sheet and aiming her gun at me. Her lips and chin trembling as tears welled in those hazel eyes.

She was so beautiful in that moment. A fierce yet vulnerable woman. If I didn't know what I wanted in a wife before then, I knew as I walked out that door and left her behind.

"What's gotten into you?" Eric says as he enters our apartment.

We've been back only a few days from the extraction we were called away for. Hopefully this time we'll get to have a real rest. A part of me wants to run to Ireland to make things right with Cass. However, gauging from her anger, I don't think that's a great idea. I plan to give the lass time.

"Nothing," I murmur.

"Then why have you been sitting around looking like someone pissed in your Cheerios for the last three days. As a matter of fact, you had that look throughout the entire mission. Actually, since we left Ireland. You were really into that chick, weren't you?"

"I've had a lot on my mind that's all."

"Bullshit, Sasha told me she called you to hook up, but she said you blew her off. No matter what's going on between you and Sasha, not once have you turned her down. You spend more time in my sister's bed than her sheets."

I heave a breath of frustration. I was tempted to hook up with Sasha when she called, but I remembered my time with Cass. I've never had that type of connection with Sasha. Great sex doesn't equate to the soul deep connection I felt with Cassie in less than one week.

"Did you need something?"

"We were supposed to go to that street festival, remember?" Eric says and pats his stomach.

"Oh yeah."

I had totally forgotten. I run a hand through my hair. I'm not in the mood to stroll the streets, eating my fill in greasy street cart food. I'd much rather stay here and lick my wounds. Hoping a certain redheaded lass will finally return my calls.

"Sasha will be here any minute. I'm going to take a leak and then head down. If you decide you want to go. We'll be waiting in case you change your mind. We'll give you a few minutes to meet up with us before we leave."

I shake my head as I frown. I forgot Sasha was supposed to join us today. Yes, we're still friends, but somehow, I feel like I'm betraying Cassie. I get the feeling the wee lass wouldn't like me running around town with an ex of mine.

Eric scoffs. "I knew you would bail, you jive ass turkey," he murmurs under his breath.

Cassie

I don't know why I'm so nervous as we walk the sidewalk leading us to the apartment building Joe lives in. I'm not sure if it's because I've come to America to tell this man he has left me with his babe. Or it could be the last time I saw him I threatened him with a shotgun and threw him out. I'm not sure I'm welcomed here.

Then there's the fact he's been calling, this should give me hope. However, I've been ignoring every single one of his calls. I wring my hands in front of me as Ronan walks beside me.

A gorgeous brown skinned woman catches my attention as we draw closer to the front entrance of the building we're going to. She has a pristine Afro that halos around her head. She's tall and her hot pants fit snug on her round hips.

Her breasts are large and put emphasis on the halter top she's wearing. As if the fabric is floating on its own, creating the perfect silhouette. She looks like she could be a model or an actress. Foxy Brown pops into my head.

We reach the entrance at the same time. Both she and I go to turn the knob simultaneously. My already frazzled nerves make my stomach reel.

"Oh sorry," I say.

"No, it's fine. Let me get that," she says with a sexy smoky voice.

"Thank ya."

She steps back out of the way and gives Ronan a lust filled look, not knowing the lad isn't more than a boy. A handsome boy, but a boy nonetheless. My brother ever the flirt, looks back at her with an alluring grin. Maybe Da should have sent one of me other brothers with me. One less interested in finding his next shag.

"Are you guys new to the building, I've never seen you before?" she asked not taking her gaze off Ronan.

"No, we're here to see a friend."

She gives us a funny look. "Your friend wouldn't happen to be Joseph Black, would it?"

"Aye, it would."

I elbow Ronan for giving information away to this stranger. He looks down at me with a scowl. I don't care, he's putting the father of my child in danger by just giving information away about where we're going. We don't know this woman.

However, I don't think the rage and fury I'm feeling are because of Ronan. It's directed more toward this woman who knows the father of my child. I want to know how she knows him, and why she's here?

"Cool, I'm headed up to his place now. Love the accents by the way. I always dig when Joe's comes out."

I ball my fist at my sides. That's the last thing I wanted to hear. Just the thought of Joe next to this gorgeous woman has my blood boiling.

I can't take my eyes off her. She starts to walk up the stairs and her shapely bottom comes into view. Her hips sway as she walks. Her legs look longer with each step. I can't help reaching for my bangs and smoothing a hand over them, then fluffing the rest. What will Joe see when he looks between the two of us?

I placed a hand over my stomach trying to calm my nerves. Before arriving here, I didn't realize how much I was willing to fight for this man. Something I thought I'd never be willing to do for anyone.

However, as I think of my child's future, I know I'll fight to the end. I began to size her up instead of standing in awe of her.

We arrive at Joe's floor, and she pulls a key from her pocket. My head nearly bursts. This was a bad idea. Why did I come here?

"Come on in," she says as if this is her place.

Ronan and I walk in behind her. Joe's friend he brought to Ireland comes and pulls the beauty into his embrace. I relax just a bit.

That's until Joe appears. She steps out of the other guy's hold. Walks over to Joe, cups his cheek, and kisses it. I see red. Joe turns to me with a look of surprise on his face. My fists are clutched so tightly, my nails bite into my skin.

"Cassie, you're here," Joe croons and come to lift me into a hug.

I'm still fuming until he puts me down and grasps my face to pull it to him for a passionate kiss. I melt into him like butter on bread.

He breaks the kiss and places his forehead to mine. "Hello, love. You're more beautiful than I remember."

"Hello, I'm Sasha. Eric's sister and Joe's girlfriend. And you are?"

My fury returns. I place my hands on my hips and lift my head.

"My Ex," Joe corrects, sending her a glare.

"My name is Cassie. I'm the mother of his child. Soon to be Cassie Black."

Joe

I think the room spins a few times and my heart explodes with it. Did she just say what I think she said? She's pregnant and she's here. I know I should be happy, but guilt fills me.

Did she really choose to come to me? Or has she come because I've saddled her with my bairn? My stomach sinks. I knew I shouldn't have done things this way. She has every right to resent me.

When I look to Sasha, I see nothing but pain on her face. I'm not sure why. We agreed to be friends and nothing more. Although, when I turn my gaze to Eric, he looks like his head is ready to burst.

"If you all will excuse us. My fiancée and I need to go have a talk," I say and place a hand on the small of Cassie's back.

I lead her through the apartment to my room. Everyone else is forgotten. Once I close the door behind us, I cup the back of her neck and bring her into to me, crushing my lips to hers.

I kiss her breathless, making up for the four and a half months we've been apart. I need to make sure she's real, she's really here. I deepen the kiss and pull her closer to me. My growing length presses into her protruding belly, which serves to remind me my seed is in there.

"How are you feeling?" I ask as I break the kiss, still holding her closes.

"Better this month," she replies. She looks down at her feet in a shy gesture that's so unlike her.

"What is it, love?"

"Who is she? Why is she here? Is she the reason you ran off?"

"She's my best friend's sister. We all had plans to go out to the street fair. I'd just begged off before you walked through the door. And I told you the reason I had to leave was because I was called onto an assignment."

She looks up at me with tears in her eyes. "Now what? If you don't want us, I'll go back to Ireland. I can raise this babe on my own."

"Don't be daft, love. You and my child aren't going anywhere. It was only a matter of time before I came for you."

I take a step back to look at her. She takes my breath away. Her face is a little bit fuller, and her cheeks are glowing. Pregnancy looks good on her.

"Da said to come to you. Is this what you really want?"

My heart sinks. She didn't come on her own. Her father sent her. I was afraid of that.

"I should be asking you that question. If you weren't pregnant, would you be here?"

"I don't know, Joe. I still don't know how I feel about ya leaving. I understand that ya had to. The timing just seemed a little too perfect to give ya an escape."

"But I've called every day. Can't you see I've grown feelings for you. If I didn't have to go, I wouldn't have."

She's silent for a moment giving me a chance to appraise her. She's wearing a cream-colored baby doll shirt with baby blue embroidery around the square neckline. Over a pair of short shorts. She looks delectable.

Her hair even seems to be more glossy than it had been when we met. I want to run my hands through it, while she writhes beneath me in ecstasy. Images of our time together assault me. It's been way too long since the last time I had her in my arms.

"Feelings? Ya have feelings for me?"

"Aye, love." I fall back into my native tongue as her emotion filled voice pulls at me.

As I stand there, it seems I might actually be making a breakthrough. If she can trust me, we can make this work. Just when I feel like I'm making headway, a knock comes at the door.

Sasha's voice floats into the room. "Joe, we're heading out to the fair. Your little friend's brother says he's going to come with us. You guys can meet up with us there. You remember our favorite place. We'll check back there periodically for you guys."

I have to wrap my arms around Cass's waist as her face clouds over and she tries to storm for the door. I place my lips to her ear. "Calm down, love. Ye are the one carrying my wee 'un. Ye are the one with my heart."

Cassie

I struggle against his hold until his last words sink in. His heart? I'm reminded he said he has feelings for me. Joe is all I've been able to think about.

It's only my stubbornness that wouldn't allow me to answer his calls. I've missed him something terrible. Even before I learned of the baby, I longed to see him again.

"Who's ya little friend? She can't be talking about me. I'm about to be yer *wife*. Is she going to be a problem, Joe? Because I'm a problem solver," I snap. "Little friend. I'll show her a little friend. I will."

"Breathe for me, Cass. Remember the baby."

He palms my little baby bump and wraps a hand around my throat and gives a gentle squeeze as he kisses the top of my head. I still for a moment. A little shocked by the gesture.

"Focus on me, love," he murmurs.

I go to protest, but he turns me and pins me to the door. His hand still around my neck. He crowds my space, closing the gap between us.

When he takes my lips and lifts me onto his waist, all else is forgotten. I push my fingers into the thick waves on top of his head.

He grunts and reaches for my hands to pin them both over my head against the door behind me. I'm lost in my want for him as he starts to grind his hips into me.

I've dreamed about his touch almost every night since he left. He releases my hand to reach for my shorts to open them before sliding them off and lowering to the floor on his knees in front of me. My feet hit the floor and I become self-conscious. My body has changed.

Seeing his perfect ex makes me question myself. However, the moment he tosses my knickers over his shoulder and lifts my leg over the other, I forget all self-doubt.

Joe makes love to my core with his mouth. I hold onto his shoulders for support as my leg begins to shake. He doesn't ease up, instead he seems to push in deeper and more rigorously with his tongue and face.

I look down my body to lock eyes with him and the intensity seems to ramp up. Soon I'm exploding as I writhe against the door, calling out his name.

I'm giddy with anticipation when the sound of his belt clinking fills the air. He lifts to his full height, never taking his eyes off me. He crushes his lips to mine. My juices are all over his mouth and face, giving me a taste of myself.

Swiftly, he lifts me onto his waist. I wrap my legs around him. Then cry out when he drives into me. I can't help but cling to his broad shoulders as he nails me to the door.

"Oh God, Joe. I've missed ya so much."

He chuckles. "Could've fooled me," he says and groans. "Ye belong to me, Cass. Don't forget that."

I bury my face in his neck, sucking my lip into my mouth to stifle my whimpers. He bends his knees and bounces me harder on his length. I gush all over the place as he slips out and my juices spray him and the floor.

Joe releases a deep groan, quickly placing his shaft back inside me. Immediately, I begin to convulse. Soaking his shaft and balls again. He moves to bite down on the side of my neck. Then licks and soothes the area before sucking it into his mouth.

Right when I think he's going to have mercy on me as he pulls away from the door and pulls out of me, he turns from the door, places me on my feet and turns me around. Joe makes quick work of pulling my shirt over my head. Then he reaches for my arms, pulling them behind me and thrusts back inside.

I cry out not able to control it any longer. He has me sobbing his name. I can't say that I regret this trip. I savor the delicious feel of him moving inside.

"God, love. I've been wanting to be back inside you for months. I plan to fuck the stubbornness right out of you," he says through clenched teeth.

"Good luck," I whimper.

Wrong move with this big lad. He releases my arms and dips to place his arms behind my knees. Bending me, he reaches between my legs and hooks his hand behind my head, lifting me off my feet. My yelp is quickly cut off by my screams of pleasure as he pounds into me while I'm folded like a pretzel.

He chuckles again. "Where's ye cheeky mouth now?"

All I can do is cry out as he drills into me. I roll my eyes in the back of my head. "Oh my God."

There's so much power in this man. I can't say I won't enjoy being married to him. If this is what it will be like. I might remain barefoot and pregnant.

If his little friend is still outside the door. I'm sure she's getting an earful. I get a little louder just in case.

CHAPTER NINE

Still Falling

Joe

"All ye have to do is decide where you want to get married. We can do it here in L.A. or you can choose between Scotland and Ireland. It's your choice," I murmur against her shoulder.

She turns in my embrace to look up at me. Those pretty hazel eyes sparkling. I can't help but peck her lips.

"Are we going to live here with yer roommate and yer ex who has a key?"

I sigh. "No. Like I told you before, I've been looking at houses in a new development with a few friends. I just haven't had time to purchase. We've all been deciding on buying homes there. I can purchase the model home that way you don't have to wait for the new build. I'll make sure we have a home before the baby gets here."

She reaches up and cups my cheek. A bright smile comes to her face. "Will there be a yard? I want to make sure the baby has some place to play."

"The lots are pretty decent we'll have more than enough yard. I believe each home has about an acre to an acre and a half."

"That sounds grand."

"We'll make it grand. I'm working with a friend to start my own company, you and the baby won't want for anything. I'm going to take care of you, Cass."

I rest a hand on her baby bump in promise to my little one, I will always be there for him or her. Cass releases a heavy sigh. A relieved look comes to her face. I thread my brows, before lifting one in question.

"I was concerned about coming here. I know ya've been calling, but ya didn't know I was pregnant then. It's a relief to see ya accept us. It seems ya have been thinking and planning for this. Ya want me here," she says.

I cup her face and take her lips in a deep kiss. I more than want her here. I've been thinking more and more about what I would change to have a family.

I've talked with my best friend, Rob. He's ready to make some changes in his life. It only makes sense we purchase homes in a family friendly neighborhood. That way if something were to happen to either of us, the other could take care of our family.

"Ye have been on my mind for four months." I leave out the fact that I've been waiting for her to arrive with news of our child.

She punches me in the shoulder. "So how long do ya plan to take to tell me the truth?"

My eyes grow wide. I'm not sure what she means, and I don't want to put a foot in my mouth. We're getting along. She's opening up to me.

"Ach, ye think me daft don't ye. Me Da told me what he told ye to do. I see yer just as ruthless as the man. Get me pregnant so I have to marry ye?" she fumes.

I don't miss the fact that her Northern Irish accent now sounds a lot more like my Scottish one. My heart warms and races at the same time. I never want to lie to her.

"I'm sorry, love. At the time, I wasn't thinking straight. I wanted you and the thought of you carrying my child, then showing up on my doorstep sent fire through my veins."

She snuggles into my side. "Remember. I only slept with ya because ya promised ya would be my husband. I was angry at first, but I got over it. Tell me, what kind of business are we starting?"

"We?" I chuckle and caress her belly. "We are starting a bounty hunting and security firm."

I expect her to give me a look of concern. Instead, her eyes light up with excitement.

"I'm marrying James Bond?"

This time I roar with laughter. I tug her into my chest as I laugh. Her stomach growls silencing me. We've been holed up in this room for hours. I've been getting reacquainted with Cass and have been hesitant to end our conversation to move, in fear of this bubble bursting.

"I need to feed my family," I say.

Reluctantly, I release her and move to get out of bed. I tug on a pair of sweats. Once decent, I head out to the kitchen.

I rummage through the refrigerator, looking to see what we have that I can make quickly. A few seconds later the sound of feet shuffling reaches my ears. I turn to find Cass sliding onto one of the stools tucked into the kitchen island. She runs a hand through her hair to push it out of her face as she watches me.

She looks adorable in my shirt that's swallowing her. I give her a wink and return to my task. I have a few steaks that were marinating. I can make her some potato cakes as well.

With a plan in mind, I get the pots and pans set up. Then get the steaks salted and seasoned and into a pan with butter, garlic, and some twined thyme and rosemary.

Cass watches me in silence. It's too quiet for me. I set the potatoes aside and move to the records and record player. I dig through the crate until I found the album I'm looking for.

I pull the record with a smile and place it on a player. The record crackles before the voice of Janis Joplin fills the apartment. I bob my head and dance my way over to the island where Cassie sits.

She has a beaming smile on her face when I reach her. I hold out my hand for her to take. She places her small palm in mine and lifts from the stool. I pull her close into me and start to dance her around the small living room.

She tilts her head to the side as she studies me. I can see the question in her eyes. I spin her out and then pull her back into my chest. I rock us from side to side and guide her hips to move with mine.

For a moment we're in our own little world. That's until the front door opens and my friends spill into the apartment. At first, I ignore them. Giving Cass one more spin. When she stiffens as I bring her into my chest, I know the dance is over. I release her so she can return to her seat.

I turn to face my friends, I find not only Eric, Ronan, and Sasha, but Steve, Rob, and Chase as well. They all gather round the living room. Sasha grabs Ronan by the hand and starts to dance with him in the middle of the space.

I purse my lips. Sasha's acting very much out of character. I don't mind she's flirting with Ronan. The kid's head is swelling from the attention. What I do mind is she seems to be taunting Cassie while she's doing it.

I'm almost tempted to throw her out and I probably would if I didn't think it would cause a problem between me and one of my best friends.

My good mood is shattered. I return to the kitchen and focus on cooking. I can't help but notice Cass keeps running a nervous hand through her hair. It's unlike the young woman I met in that house party. I prefer the feisty in your face version of Cassidy.

Then it hits me, I've yet to introduce her to my friends.

"Rob, Steve, Chase, I want you to meet someone. Cass, these are my best friends and hopefully our future neighbors," I say with a broad grin on my face. "Guys, this is Cassidy, my fiancée and the mother of my first born."

"Whoa, when did this happen?" Rob says.

"Four months ago, while I was in Ireland."

"A lot happened on that trip we don't know about," Chase says.

"It's nice to meet you, Cassie." Rob is the first to say. "Congratulations on the engagement and the baby."

"Thank ya," Cass says.

"When's the wedding?" Steve asks.

"We're still working that out. First, we need to decide where we want to have it," I reply.

"I'm thinking Scotland," Cass says and my heart swells.

I was willing to get married in Ireland, but I was hoping she would choose Scotland. I would love for her to get to see my home.

"If that's your wish, it's my command," I say.

"Isn't your sister and her husband moving back to Ireland?" Steve asks.

"That was the word the last time I talked to Da. They should be settling in this month. I'm going to be an uncle again. So, they're in a hurry to get into their new place, before Dougie has to get back to business," I say.

"Will he be coming to the States for his father again?" Eric asks.

"I believe so. He wants Kara and Logan to come with him. So, we'll have to plan our wedding around their trip."

"Would it be better to marry here?"

"No, love. We can marry wherever you like."

Cassie

His words place a sour look on Sasha's face. She has been watching Joe like a hawk. She glares at me when I cover my baby bump protectively.

If she wants a fight, I'm still capable of cobbling her. Joe must pick up on the tension. He moves his gaze to her then back to me.

"Cass and I will be moving out soon," he says. "I'll help you find a new roommate if you need."

"It's all right. Sash can move in. It will save me money. That dorm is expensive," Eric says. "Congratulations, by the way. You look happy."

"I am," Joe says.

Suddenly, that's all I need. I unclench my fists and rest my hands in my lap. I've fallen in love with this man. I don't need to fight for what I already have.

Joe

I'm headed to the bathroom when a hand lands on my shoulder. I look behind me to see Sasha bouncing from foot to foot. Looking nervous and… hurt?

"What's up?" I ask.

"You're really going to marry her. How do you know it's your baby? You haven't seen her in months."

I lower my voice. "Because not everyone's you. I can trust her," I snarl.

She jerks her head back as if struck. "Wow, Joe."

"Wow, Sasha. *You* said we could be friends. *You* said you were fine with moving on. *You* were the one to cheat on me. While I had pussy being thrown at me left and right. I was faithful to you.

"Now, I'm happy and moving on and you want to be all in your feelings. Save it. Either go out there and show Cass some respect or say your goodbyes right here. She's going to be my wife and she's having my baby. This ship has sailed. We're over. I've fallen for someone else. There's nothing you can say to change that."

"Sash," Eric calls to his sobbing sister.

"I'm sorry. I never meant to lose you. You were so angry when I first told you. I had to say something, so you didn't walk out on me. I thought I had time to make it right."

"Sash, let this go."

"Wait, Eric. I can't leave him so angry with me. I was wrong. He's a good man and I fucked up. It's not her fault, it's mine. I just need to know he can forgive me. I don't want to lose my friend," she sobs.

I pull her into a hug. "You won't lose me if you can respect my relationship. She's important to me. She's the one. She's worthy."

"Then make her your own." Sasha smiles up at me. I once told her those words that were said to me as a young lad. Her response shows me she remembers them.

I look over her head to see Cass staring at us, working her jaw. I release Sash and she turns toward Cass. I brace myself. Not sure what either will do. Both Sasha and Cass are hotheads, not to mention Sash can be darn right petty.

Sasha walks over to Cass and pulls her into an embrace.

"He's an amazing guy. You're so lucky. I'm so sorry for my behavior. Congratulations. I hope we can become friends. I'm a great babysitter." I sigh in relief when Cass returns the hug.

"I'm open to being friends, but you so much as breathe wrong in my husband's direction, I'm going to teach ya a lesson ya won't forget," Cass says with a straight face.

"I like you already," Sash says.

CHAPTER TEN

Our New Life

Joe

A year and four months later…

Smokey Robinson's Quiet Storm plays as I soothe my son on my bare chest. I'm bonding with my boy while Cass takes some time to herself. I sway through the living room and stop before the mantel to stare at the picture frame in the center.

It's of our wedding day. Cass was unbelievably gorgeous in the cream lace gown with the square neckline that showed off her swollen cleavage. It sinched right under her breasts, allowing the fabric to flow over her post pregnancy belly.

Cass was self-conscious as she had just given birth a little over a month before. It took nearly six months from the time she showed up on my doorstep before we were able to get married. It was the soonest we were able to get everyone to Scotland.

"That was the best day of my life until you were born," I say to Wyatt before kissing the top of his brown waves.

He bounces in my arms and drools all over my chest. The lad is tall and already moving out of the way for his brother or sister. Cass is expecting again, and I couldn't be happier.

This house is big enough for us to have more than a few more. I already started painting the new nursey. Since we don't know if it's a boy or girl, I went with a light gray Cass loves.

Wyatt squeals in my arms, causing me to look up. Cass walks in with Sasha dancing in behind her. Cass and Sasha have become great friends and Wyatt adores Sash. My lad is going to be a breast man. Without fail, every time, the moment she picks him up, his head is rested on her chest and his little hand is stuck between her cleavage.

Sasha adores him just as much. She spoils him rotten. Immediately, she comes and plucks him from my arms. Wyatt's entire face lights up and his head goes to her breasts.

Sasha cups the back of his head and sways with him. "How's my handsome, sweet boy?" she coos to him.

He lifts his head as if he can talk and replies with some gibberish. Sasha laughs and takes a seat on the couch with him still in her arms.

I dance my way over to Cass and take her into my arms from behind. I place my hands on her protruding belly and kiss her neck. In no time, I'm swaying us both to the music as she sags into me.

"Hello, love. I've missed you. Did you guys have a good time?"

"Did I empty out the store, buying baby clothes? Aye, yes, I did."

I chuckle and throw my head back. She's been nesting. I believe it's worse this time than it was with Wyatt. Wyatt's cry fills the room, I look up from Cass and my son has tears in his golden eyes as he pulls a long face.

"I think someone's hungry," Sash says. "Do you have milk pumped? I'll feed him."

Cass groans. "No, I'll do it. I didn't get to pump much this morning. Joe probably went through all that was left."

"We did. I was hoping you were on your way back," I say.

Cass takes the baby and heads upstairs, I'm sure to her favorite feeding spot.

Wyatt looks huge in her arms. I can't help but wonder how things will be when she has two and I'm away. Sasha pulls me from my thoughts.

"I see you worrying. Cass is strong and a good mom. She'll be fine. Besides, I'll be around," she says. She tilts her head to the side studying me. "Are you heading out with Eric this time?"

I wrinkle my brows. I haven't been called in and as far as I know neither has the rest of the team.

"No, not this time," I reply.

"That's odd. This is the third assignment in six months he's been on without you," she muses.

I don't say it, but I'm thinking the same thing. It's not unusual for us to be called on different assignments based on our expertise. However, as Eric's commander, I'm finding this to be interesting.

It's very likely he's taking on some private sector work. Which he doesn't have to share with me. In fact, it's better if he doesn't. Yet, I'm still a bit curious.

Curious, not concerned—yet. Eric has been acting a bit differently. At first, I thought it might have been because Rob and I officially started to set up Black and Lock. We had invited him in, but he wasn't interested at the time.

Sash waves it off. "He's probably seeing someone new." She shrugs. "You know how he likes dating them ugly girls and then gets mad at me when I point out to him how ugly they are, and he realizes it for himself."

I can't help it, I roar with laughter. Just then Cass returns with Wyatt looking fed, changed, and happy as he suckles from his mother's breast.

I grab Cass and nuzzle her neck, envious of my son. I always desire my wife, but there's something about seeing her take care of our lad that gets me every time.

"Well, that's my cue. Cass, I'll get your things out of my car and into the nursery for you before I pull off."

"Joe can do it."

I head for my shirt and shoes without asking any questions. When I get to the car, I'm not sure they left anything in the store. My chest swells with pride. My children will want for nothing. I'm glad Cass was able to shop to her heart's desire.

Cassie

I look down at my sweet boy as he stares up at me while he fills his belly and clenches my breast tightly. His brother or sister kicks him from within my womb. Wyatt only wiggles a little before settling back as he continues to suck happily.

I brush a finger over his forehead and curls. He blinks his long stunning lashes at me. I sigh and shake my head.

"Ye will be a heartbreaker." I laugh at myself as I find my words sounding more and more like Joe's each day. My brothers have threatened to bring me home, so I'll stop talking like a Scot.

"I wouldn't have it. This is where we belong, isn't it?" I coo to my boy.

I think Joe is hoping for another boy. I'm starting to think he might be right. Four brothers, three with children and not one girl in sight. My chances for a girl are looking slim.

I adore Joe's niece. She gives me hope. Her brother Logan pops into my mind, and I smile broader at Wyatt.

"If all ye gets is brothers, they sure have good genes. They'll all be as handsome as you. I'll be mounting me guns over the door before this one gets here."

Wyatt stops sucking and seems to laugh at me. "I'm not joking. I can see it now, little fire crouches lined up at me door. Mrs. Black is Wyatt home?"

My babe in the womb, kicks as if in agreement with me. "See, yer brother knows."

"So, you believe it's a boy?"

I look up to find Joe standing in the doorway with his arms folded across his chest. He looks at me with fire in his eyes. No wonder I was pregnant almost as soon as this one popped out. My husband is insatiable.

Not even a wee bairn and pregnancy has slowed him down. I'm not complaining. The man is amazing in bed. I don't need anything to compare him to. I'm quite sure no other man can do the things Joe does.

"Aye, I do believe it's another boy."

He saunters over and takes a seat beside me on the sofa, placing his arm behind me, across the back of the sofa. I look up at him as Wyatt plays with my pinky.

Joe plants a quick kiss on my lips. Then raises a brow. "Shall we choose a name then?

"I was thinking. Seamus."

Joe groans and shakes his head. He places his hand on my belly. "I won't let you do that to my lad. How about Noah?"

I think it over for just a second. However, our little one seems to like the name as he gives me a swift double kick.

Joe winks at me. "He likes it. If it's a boy. Noah it is."

CHAPTER ELEVEN

Clean Up

Cassie

Six years later...

I hold Felix on my hip as I hold John's little hand and he toddles on his little legs. We're heading for the picnic table in the center of the yard where everyone's waiting for us to sing happy birthday.

I can't believe Wyatt is already six and we have another on the way. All of our friends are here, and a few family members have come in from Ireland and Scotland. Wyatt's little cousins sit around with excited faces covered in frosting from cupcakes. Today has turned out to be an awesome day.

Halfway to table Sasha appears with Wyatt in her arms as she tickles him. His laughter pierces the yard as his little cheeks glow with happiness.

He gives her a bright smile before placing his head on her chest. Wyatt and his godmother have a special bond. He always gets excited to see her. Sometimes, it feels like she's more protective of him than I am.

She tosses him in the air, causing him to giggle as she catches him. He gives her that lady killer smile, I swear, Joe is teaching to all of my sons.

"He's playing ye," I warn.

"It's okay. The kid knows I'd die for him. Isn't that right, handsome?"

Wyatt's face brightens. "Yup, Tee-tee Sasha." He laughs out in his little voice and giggles, smushing her face between his hands.

I laugh and shake my head starting toward the table to rest my feet. I've been on them all day and with this little one growing so quickly within my belly, I need a break.

Joe and these big boys are going to break my back. Yes, this time we found out the sex of the baby early. In hopes it would be a girl. No such luck, we'll be having our fifth boy. Toby it will be.

I'm excited. Wyatt, Noah, and John are already so close. Every time I turn around Noah is trying to chase after his older brother. The two are pretty much inseparable. Many think they're twins. Irish twins yes, although they look identical, they're a year apart. Noah is a big lad for his age.

Johnathan is a more reserved child. He reasons everything even at his young age. He reminds me of Joe with his level headedness.

Joe storms out of the house with a grim look on his face, contradicting the thought I just had. I pinch my brows wondering what's going on. Shortly after Rob, Steve, Chase, and Eric all follow out behind him.

The first thing I note is Joe's hustler. He doesn't usually wear it when home around the children. He looks dangerous and sexy in jeans and a polo with black boots on his feet. Eric seems to try to get Joe's attention, but Joe is fuming. He shrugs Eric off and comes to pluck Wyatt from Sasha's arms. I get a sinking feeling in my stomach.

Sasha frowns but catches herself before she reaches for Joe's arm. She looks to me and takes Felix from my hold.

"Is everything okay, Joe?" I ask as I wrap my arms around his waist.

He nods his head curtly and purses his lips. From the dip in his brow, I can tell how angry he is, which is why he doesn't give me a verbal reply.

I look across to Eric who's watching Joe closely. "I might need to send ye and the boys away for a bit," Joe finally says tightly. Yup, he's angry, not a hint of his American accent can be heard.

I snap my head back toward my husband. "What? Why?"

"Because I have friends who don't think," he says bitterly. "I need my family safe while I clean up their mess. I've talked to yer brothers. They agree with me it's time to put Kasey to bed.

"This new development makes him a problem. Ye, Sasha, and the lads should take a trip. Ronan will go with ye all."

Ronan has been spending a lot of time in the States since turning twenty. I'm not complaining. I love having my little brother here with me.

"I'll be fine right here in my home. I know how to take care of myself."

Joe palms the back of my neck and places his forehead to mine. "But that's not what I need. I need ye and my boys safe. Yer pregnant and we have four small lads. You can't wield your shotguns with John and Felix on your hips. I promised I'd always keep you safe. Allow me to do that.

"Your brothers and I will handle this. I need to burn this hornet's nest down and then ye can come back home," Joe says with so much emotion clinging to his voice.

"What does Kasey have to do with Eric?"

Joe scowls. His face turning red. "Dad," Wyatt says, bringing a smile back to his father's face.

Joe runs a hand over his waves. Seeming to sense his father's anger, Wyatt places a hand on Joe's cheeks. Joe turns his head and starts to nibble on his fingers, drawing a giggle from our sweet little one.

"He's been taking side jobs," Joe says to me as he tickles Wyatt to keep him squealing. "Apparently, he was hired only to be followed back here to the States. Kasey now knows how to find you and has sent me and my team a threat," he says with heat I know isn't directed toward me.

"Why now? It's been years. Can't the fat fuck take a hint. I don't want him. He should spend more time washing his ass, instead of looking for me," I fume.

"Oliver Kasey Sr. was killed a few months ago. The son is now running things and he's still bent out of shape about me taking you."

I snort. "I probably wouldn't have been able to find his pecker under all those grease stains. The man smelled like ass and old lard. I wasn't going to allow him to paw on me, he might as well get over it."

Joe booms with laugher. Mission accomplished. I hate seeing him this upset. Especially not on our son's birthday.

"So, when do we leave?" I say when his laughter dies down.

He leans in to kiss my lips. "In the morning. I'm sending you to the beach house. The boys will have fun there."

"Oh, great, I'll have time to put up those new curtains."

He frowns. "I told you, I'd do it the next time we head there. It can wait for me."

I roll my eyes. "Toby will be here before ye have time to do it for me. I got it, love, but thank ye."

Joe smiles when he hears his angry accent has rubbed off on me.

CHAPTER TWELVE

Ultimate Sacrifice

Cassie

We've been at the beach house for two weeks. When I talk to Joe, he sounds exhausted and frustrated. I'm also starting to feel like he isn't telling me everything.

The boys miss him and so do I. Sasha wants to get back to her life and I can't blame her. Being stuck with me and my little brats can't be ideal.

I walk through the house with Felix on my hip as I look for everyone else. I've just awoken from a much-needed nap. This pregnancy has been kicking my arse. I don't know if it's because I'm already chasing after four or if this little fucker in here is determined to give me hell, but it seems like my energy is always tapped.

I find Ronan on the couch with John on his chest, both out for the count. Laughter from outside causes me to look out the window. Sash has Wyatt and Noah on the Big Wheels she bought for them.

"Spoiled brats," I mutter to myself.

They're riding around the driveway, chasing after each other as Sash cheers them on. Noah's little cheeks are red as he works his legs to catch up to his brother. John stirs from his sleep, waking Ronan as well.

"Hey, *siúr*," Ronan says sheepishly. I pluck John up before he can make a fuss.

"Hey, don't sister me. Falling asleep on the job, you slacker?"

He rubs the back of his neck and blushes. "He fell asleep first. I didn't want to wake you and Felix. So I kept him with me and nodded off."

"Aye, sure he did." I twist my lips and side eye Ronan.

"I'm going to take a quick shower," he says.

I look to John. "Want to go outside?" I coo to him and Felix.

John gives me a shy smile and nods his head sleepily. Felix only watches me as he always does. I wonder what goes on that little head of his.

He's a bright boy. His eyes are sharp, and he seems to always be assessing the situation. With Felix on my hip and John's little hand in mine, I head outside. The sun is baking. I'll burn if I sit out here too long. I opt to sit on the covered porch in the shade on the swing Joe added just for days like this.

The beach house was a gift from Joe. We've enjoyed it over the years, although I have a few renovations I've been after Joe about.

"You look rested," Sash says as she comes to take a seat with me.

"That nap was just what I needed," I say, releasing John and Felix as they go to play with their little cars on the mat we set up on the porch.

"I'm going to order some pizza if that's cool with you. The boys keep asking me too. I told them I'd check with you once you were up."

"It's fine. I'm not in the mood to cook anyway. I could use the break."

"I'm here to help," she says before releasing a heavy breath.

I turn to observe her. Although she looks happy and gorgeous with her long braids and the pretty beads at the ends, something has been off. She's been a bit distant.

"What be on ye mind?" I ask.

She turns to look at me with a little smile. "I met someone," she replies. "He asked me to move to New York with him."

"So, it's serious then?"

"Yeah, I guess it is. I'm not about to mess up another good thing."

"Poor Wyatt will be devastated," I tease.

"I know. It's one of the reasons I'm reluctant."

"Oh, please, the lad will get over it. You go on and live your life. We can come to New York, or you can come in for the holidays."

"Are you kidding? I'll be here for every holiday, birthday, graduation. I want to vet every little girlfriend they have." She laughs.

"In that case, you'll be pretty busy. I have a feeling these little fuckers are going to give me and Joe a run for our money."

"I have no doubt they will. Did you see the little one up the street giving Wyatt the look from under her lashes?" she asks with a chuckle.

"I did. I told her mum, I did." I join her in laughter as Felix tries to climb onto my lap. "No, seriously, love. I'm happy for you. Do what's best for you. What does Eric think?"

She chews on her lip. "I haven't had time to talk to him about it. We're all we have. When our parents died, Eric took me in and made sure I had everything I needed. I'll be sad to leave him, but he's been changing on me. I think some time apart will be good. I miss my brother," she says.

"Eric has had a lot on his plate. I'm sure he'll come around. Maybe some time would be good."

Something flashes our way from the street. Sash looks out toward the road. She narrows her eyes and stands.

"That car, it's been sitting there all day. At first, I thought they were here for the neighbors, but something is funky with them. They keep watching us."

I follow her line of sight. The men seem to home in on us. My hackles go up. I tighten my hold on Felix and pull him close.

"Boys, come here," Sasha calls to Wyatt and Noah. They both turn to her and start to ride closer to us.

"Cass, get your gun," she says right before she takes off running. The car starts and heads for our driveway.

It all happens so quickly. Sasha reaches the boys just before the car hops the curb and careens into our driveway. I'm paralyzed with shock.

One moment I'm talking with one of my best friends. The next she's pinned under a car after saving two of my son's lives. I hold Felix tightly to my chest as reality starts to set in.

"Tee-tee Sasha," Wyatt sobs loudly.

It clicks in my brain Wyatt is hollering at the top of his lungs as he brushes Sasha's beaded hair from her face as if trying to wake her from sleep. Noah stands beside them with his fists balled and a scowl on his face.

The car door opens. I snap into action running for my boys. The man who steps out isn't as tall as Joe, but he's a tall man. Another guy steps out of the other side.

He's not as big, but I'm ready to take them both on if I have to. I get to Wyatt and help him up by grabbing his hand. Noah is still glaring at both men as if he's sizing them up to take them down.

"I have a message for you," the one who got out of the driver's side says.

I lift my chin and glare at him. While the two of them are focused on me, neither sees my husband storming toward us, looking like a dark avenging angel. Joe's face is clouded over with rage and a mix of other emotions.

"Tell ya husband, the Kasey family plans to collect. We'll take someone from him for every week until the debt is paid—"

Without looking, Joe places a bullet in the head of the silent man from across the car. He then places his gun with the silencer at the back of the head of the one who spoke.

"If ye have a fucking message for me, ye give it to me like a fucking man," Joe barks before pulling the trigger. The guy's head explodes before he can get to reply.

Noah runs over to the man lying at his father's feet and kicks at his torso. As if to finish the already done job. Joe scoops him up and buries Noah's face in his neck as he walks him over to me.

"Tee-tee Sasha," Wyatt whimpers.

Joe looks over to her lifeless body and I can see the hurt in his face. However, the heartbreaking moment is when Eric comes speeding around the car. It's then I notice the rest of Joe's team. I hadn't known they were so close. Last I spoke to Joe, he said they were in Ireland.

Eric releases a soul wrenching sob and drops to his knees. It's too late she's gone, but Rob, Chase, and Steve still try to lift the car off Sasha's broken body. Eric is able to pull her out and cradle her in his arms. He rocks with her in his hold as he sobs over her broken body.

"This is all my fault," he cries. "I'm so sorry, sis. I'm so sorry, Sash. I'm so sorry."

CHAPTER THIRTEEN

Memories

Joe

I can tell by the scowls on my older boy's faces. They remember their Auntie Sasha. I will forever be grateful to her for saving Wyatt and Noah.

If only we'd been a few minutes earlier. The call had come in that we should head back stateside. We were on our way back when Rob got a hit on the crew we were watching. After spilling Kasey's blood and sending a clear message back to the one I knew was behind the bank roll for Kasey's boldness, we knew they would try something.

"I remember her," Wyatt says with a grimace. "I don't remember that day though. I didn't remember that's what happened to her."

"Wow, I'm sorry," Carmen says.

"For what, lass? Our past is a part of who we are," I say.

"What happened to the person who sent those guys?" Roni asks.

"We took care of them," Ronan bites out.

I think he had a glad eye for Sasha. When he came from his shower after the attack that day, I could see the devastation on his face. He took it hard. Instead of moving to New York as he had been planning, he returned to Ireland once we straightened out our little problem.

"What happened to Uncle Eric?" John asks.

I purse my lips and look over at Cass. She gives me a small nod and reaches to squeeze my hand.

"He took Sasha's death hard. He started to drink and moved away. The guilt ate at him. I think he cleaned himself up but seeing you boys is too hard for him."

"We've invited him to every wedding. He's hasn't shown up," Cass adds.

"But isn't Uncle Eric who started my training?" Noah asks.

"Aye, he did," Ronan says. "That was before it became too much. He wanted ya to be able to protect yerselves."

"I think it was the autopsy," Ronan says, making a face as if he tastes sand. "Once he found out Sasha was carrying the babe he spiraled out. If I could kill O'Brien again, I would. We let that old bastard live far beyond his expiration date."

"You can say that again," Logan grumbles as he takes a seat.

One of my biggest regrets, was how we had to handle O'Brien. My father was firm on the fact I had to allow him to live. I've never questioned Cole on whether or not he was the one to end his grandfather's life because frankly, I don't give a fuck.

As long as the bastard is gone, I'm a happy man. Being the one to spill his blood would have been the only thing that could make me happier.

I clap my hands together. "Enough of all that. We're here to celebrate my son and daughter," I say, looking to Roni with a smile.

"So everyone here had a big formal wedding?" Carmen asks with her brows pinched.

My gaze goes straight to Ryan. I can tell he's about to blow it. Thankfully, Roni comes to the rescue. She stands and pulls Carmen from her seat, tossing Ryan a wink.

When they're gone everyone at the table roars with laughter. My laugh comes from deep. This lad is intent on ruining his own plan.

"Yer going to blow it," Ronan teases.

"I've been trying to tell him," Cass says with annoyance in her voice.

"Ya'll be giving me my airfare back if you blow this," Ronan says.

Ryan rolls his eyes. "I'm paying for all the jets and fuel, so what are ya griping about?"

I chuckle and shake my head. The lad is right, he's taking on more bounties for the extra cash. I sit back and fold my arms over my chest. I look around at my seven lads.

I'm proud of my boys. If I would have known what my father had planned for me all those years ago, I might have avoided Ireland all together.

Now as I think about it. I have loved, I have laughed, and I have lived a good life with this little woman at my side. I place a hand on the back of her neck and give a gentle squeeze. She looks up at me with a sparkle in her eyes. She smirks and lifts a brow at me.

I know that look. "We should get Mena to bed and turn in ourselves," I announce.

"Sure," Wyatt scoffs.

"Ye, mind yer own business. Ye might want to start checking a mirror after ye go for a quick shag in the coat closet," Cass snaps at him.

We all look at Wyatt with his misbuttoned shirt and rumpled hair. On cue the table erupts into laughter.

I stand and take a sleeping Mena from Cass, placing her on my shoulder. Then I wrap an arm around my wife. "You all have a good night. If we don't see you in the morning, we'll see you at the next wedding," I say.

"Don't teach my daughter anything I wouldn't," John says.

I snort. "You haven't learned the things I know, lad. You're still playing at life," I reply.

Laughter goes up and a chorus of goodnights follows after us as we leave. I catch sight of Ronan and memories seem to cling to his thoughts as he throws back a drink and looks utterly shattered. I remind myself to have a talk with my brother-in-law in the morning.

Some things we have to learn when to let go of.

CHAPTER FOURTEEN

Regrets

Ronan

Everyone at the table laughs around me. No one knowing the pain I'm in as I sit here. My past and present are making a mess of me.

I feel like an eejit. How didn't I see this sooner? I pull a face and grab my glass and the bottle of whiskey from the table. Those stories brought back old memories I didn't know I was still festering over.

Maybe my wife is right. She's not the only one with baggage. I've been after her to give us a chance, but I have demons in my closet holding me back as well.

"Hey, Uncle Ro, what's up?" Braxton asks as he walks up beside me as I make my way to the fields to clear my mind.

"Just taking a dooter. Nothing to fash yerself about."

"You thought she would be here, didn't you?"

I look my nephew in the eyes as I bite back my anger. It's not anger with him. It's anger because I've allowed this shit to get so out of hand.

"Aye, I did," I say in reply to my nephew.

My wife should be here with me. Instead, she insists on pushing me away. What I love most about her is her brilliant brain and how she's built her own. Her independence turns me on, but it gets stuck in my craw when she wields it like a weapon against me.

People have taken advantage of her giving heart and generosity and the fact she has maintained so much wealth. She pushes me away because of them.

I want nothing from my wife but her love. She'd never have to spend another dime if she'd allow me to take care of her. It took me a long time to get over Sasha and my unborn child. So yes, I can be overbearing and possessive. I was so young when I lost them.

I'm trying hard to show my wife I mean well and I'm trying to change for her. However, now when I think about it. I need to close the door to my past and stop treating my woman as if I'm going to lose her before I actually do.

"Will you be going back to New York? Does she know it's not safe to be without you? Once others find out it'll be a problem."

"Aye, she and I need to have a long talk. I don't want to live like this anymore." I take a swig from the bottle, tossing the glass aside. "I've spent years scared to love again. I'm not wasting another day. As for the threats, I'm not losing another woman I love."

Brax draws his brows in. My three younger nephews never met the amazing woman who gave her life for two of their siblings. Sash would have gone nuts over Toby and Brax's red hair. I can't help but wonder if our wee one would have inherited mine.

Closing my eyes against the thought, I then place the bottle against Braxton's chest, once he takes it, I pat his cheek. I'm proud of my nephews.

I've watched them become men and fall in love. I will always remember Sasha for her sacrifice no matter how painful it has been to mourn and live without her, I can't blame myself forever.

I hadn't known about the baby when I decided to move to American and settle in New York for good. I'd asked Sash to live with me because we fit. She was older than me, but young and fun. The most beautiful woman I'd ever seen until I met my wife.

"Set me free," I whisper into the night as I head back to the wedding.

CHAPTER FIFTEEN

A Word

Joe

I wake to the sound of my granddaughter's little voice. When I open my eyes, Mena sits on the bed by me whispering, "Grandpe Joe. Grandme, wake up. Grandpe."

I look around, wondering how she made it in between the two of us without waking us as she climbed onto the bed. Seeing I'm awake she moves to me and cups my face.

"Good morning, love."

"Grandpe," she squeals and moves to kiss my cheek. For all of Roni's lack of displays of affection Mena doesn't shy away from showing her feelings and affection.

I sit up and pull her into my arms, tickling her tummy as it growls back at me. "Are you hungry?"

She nods her head as she gives me an adorable smile. I look over to Cass, she's still out for the count. I don't expect her to wake anytime soon. Not after last night. I grin at the memories of our evening.

Shaking my head clear, I then swing my legs over the edge of the bed and get up. I scratch my belly and stretch with Mena on my hip. Thank God I put on sweats before going to sleep last night. I head into the bathroom to brush both our teeth before going downstairs.

Once done, I head down to the kitchen. Ronan sits with a cup of what smells like coffee in front of him as he holds his head. Just the person I wanted to see.

"Good morning," I murmur as I place Mena on the stool beside him.

She looks up at Ronan with a smile and places her hand on his arm. "Hi," she sings to him.

He turns his head slightly. "Hey, love. Ya mind not yelling at me, please."

I scoff. "Rough night?"

"How about rough life?"

I place a bowl of cereal in front of Mena. "Thank you."

"You're welcome, sweetheart," I reply to her and turn to Ronan. "About that, I wanted to ask you a question."

He groans. "Whatever Cass said I did, I didn't. Not this time."

"You're fine this time. My question is about our past. Your past. Were you involved with Sash before the incident?"

He looks away and runs a hand through his hair. "We started dating when I turned nineteen, before that she would flirt. I would flirt back, but I never thought I had a shot."

"But you did."

"Yeah." He shrugs and gives a hint of the cocky smile I know him for. "We kept things a secret because I didn't know how you and Cass would feel about it. We were planning to move to New York together. She wanted to tell you guys first. Then you had to take off and I… I needed a shower. It was only fifteen minutes. Fifteen minutes and they were gone. I didn't know she was pregnant. I'm not sure if she knew."

I round the counter and place a hand on his shoulder. I give a gentle squeeze. The pain in his eyes is so clear.

"She was a special person. I can't blame you for falling for her."

"I didn't realize I was still holding on to all that."

"Grief can be that way."

He snorts. "How do you grieve for thirty years?"

"It was a terrible day. It stuck with us all in some way. However, I knew Sash. She would want you to live your life. Forgive yourself. You have a life waiting on you. You couldn't have known. I tried to get there as fast as I could, but I had to forgive myself when I didn't."

He purses his lips and nods. "Thanks, Joe."

"Anytime. You know if you ever need to talk, I'm here."

I nod and turn to make breakfast for myself and Cass. "You want something to eat?"

"Does my sister curse like a sailor?"

"Aye, eggs and bacon coming up."

CHAPTER FIFTEEN

Big Dick Energy

Cassie

I stir the cabbage in the pot and go to take the biscuits out of the oven. Kamara gets the cranberry sauce onto the dish I just gave her. The other girls sit at the kitchen nook talking and tending to the wee ones.

I look up when Carmen comes storming into the kitchen with a frown on her face. Oh, for goodness's sake, not this shit again. I ought to kill Ryan.

I groan and roll my eyes. I've had about enough of Ryan and Carmen. One more month and these two will have a wedding and I can stop clenching my jaw.

Ryan keeps acting like a weirdo and Carmen, the bright girl she is, picks up on it every time. She's suspicious and none of us can blame her.

"Do you think he's cheating on me?" Carmen muses to us as she looks around the kitchen.

Nellie and Bean cover their mouths to hide their laughter. Roni rolls her eyes and heads to the dining room with the guys. I want to follow behind her myself. If I didn't think I'd burn the thanksgiving bird, I would.

Instead, I pick up the spoon I used to stir the cabbage and shake it at her. "My boys don't cheat," I scold.

"Well, he's been doing something," she mutters under her breath.

I look her attire over and lift a brow. "Is that why you're wearing that tight sweater dress and those kinky boots?"

I'd noticed the heeled boots when they arrived. I caught my son, her husband rearranging himself as she pranced away from him. No, my boy isn't cheating. He's too smitten by her.

"No," Carmen pouts but from the way her eyes shift I know she's lying.

"Wyatt and I had the room next to you guys the night before and after John's wedding. I don't think you have to worry about Ryan cheating. God, I could barely hear my own orgasms over you two," Nellie says.

"Nellie, Bean, take these biscuits and cranberry sauce out for me, please." I walk over to Carmen, grab her arm, and pull her to sit on the stool beside me as I climb up on one myself.

"I know with all me heart that boy loves you. Will you rest yer brain and give my nerves a break?"

She huffs and folds her arms over her chest. The others return and retake their seats. I can tell they're still fighting their laughter.

"Just look at them," Carmen says as she glares into the dining area. "Sitting there with all that big dick energy. Like they own the world or something."

I toss my head back and laugh so deep my belly hurts. The others lose their battle with their laughter as well. I narrow my eyes at Carmen as my brain starts to calculate as I take her in fully.

Her face is fuller, she's been extra sensitive, and she's feistier than usual. I lean into her ear. "When do you plan to tell him?" I whisper.

She turns to me with surprise in her eyes. "You know?"

"I do now."

"I'm not telling him a thing if he keeps acting like this," she mutters.

Just than Ryan enters the kitchen with their tiny monster on his hip. Her little fat brown cheeks are filled with something she's chewing on. Ryan looks nervously between myself and Carmen.

"Everything okay?" he asks.

"No everything isn't okay. You're making my butt itch with all this weirdo shit you're on. What's your problem?" Carmen hisses.

Jordan's mouth falls open to reveal a biscuit inside. She frowns at her mother and shakes her little finger at her.

Ryan cups the side of Jordan's head, covering her ear and pulls her into his chest. He looks at Carmen incredulously. She huffs and rolls her eyes.

"Sorry, baby," Ryan says. "Mommy has been grumpy all week."

"Me?"

"Yeah, you."

"I wonder why? I swear to God, if you're cheating on me, I'm going to chop your hands and your pecker off then feed them to whoever she is."

I have to say, my mouth falls open this time. I thought I could get vicious during a pregnancy. Ryan rolls his lips to keep from laughing. He then hands me the baby and cages Carmen in with his arms, his hands against the counter behind her.

"I love the ground you walk on. I'd drink every drop of your bath water on your filthiest day. I spend so much of my time watching your ass sway, I wouldn't know what another woman looks like." He kisses her nose. "I promise you on my life, you can keep your swords in the closet. I'm not cheating, and I never will."

"Then what's going on with you? The late hours, you claim to be working all the time. I found you in my closet of all places and you freaked out…" She pauses and her eyes enlarge. "Dear God, I got the crossdressing brother. It's okay, babe. If that's what you're into… just tell me. We can shop for your size. My clothes are too small for you."

We all laugh at her. Even Jordan starts to laugh as we do. Ryan cups her face while still laughing.

"I'm working extra hours for your and Jordan's Christmas gifts. I was in your closest to get your size for part of your gift. Trust me, I'm not doing anything nefarious."

Carmen bursts into tears and wraps her hands around Ryan's. "I'm sorry, this baby has me acting crazy and you're acting weird, and Jordan gives me attitude like she's thirty. I'm just overwhelmed."

This time Ryan is the one to look shocked. I grin at my boy as he pales and stares at his wife. I think it takes him a moment to remember to breathe.

"You're pregnant?" he says.

"Yeah."

Ryan lifts her from the stool and kisses the shit out of her. I cover Jordan's eyes and burst into laughter as she tries to look around my hand. I guess we know why this little one is so grown, she's getting out of the way for the next one.

"Hey, can we eat?" Noah rumbles from the dining room.

"Aye, come get the bird."

"About time," Wyatt mutters.

I wouldn't trade a single one of them. Joe looks to me and gives me a smile. The look on his face says he's thinking the same thing.

CHAPTER SIXTEEN

It's Okay

Carmen

Ryan backs me into our bedroom after we put Jordan down for the night. He has his hands on my hips as he looks down into my eyes.

Thanksgiving dinner went better than expected after I told him about the baby. I accept all his weird behavior is because of this gift he's planning. It better be one hell of a gift because he's stressing me the hell out.

"It's going to be okay," he says against my lips as if he's reading my thoughts before kissing me deeply. "I love you."

Tears spring to my eyes. I know he does. I've just been so overwhelmed. We'd planned on Jordan turning six or seven before having another baby. We both need some more time to mature. However, life doesn't seem to care or think so.

"I love you too, but your pullout game really is trash," I tease.

He laughs and pulls me into his chest for a tight hug. "Baby, you give out that cocaine pussy. Can you blame me?"

This time I laugh. I sober up. "Are you sure we're ready for another baby?"

"Ready or not, it's coming. If we're not ready, we will be by the time he or she is here. Please let it be a boy. I love Jordan, but I know she gets away with murder because she's my little princess."

"As if our son wouldn't be spoiled too. Have you met you and Brax?" I ask and roll my eyes.

He returns the gesture and backs me up into the bed. I give his chest a gentle shove and reach to pull my sweater dress over my head. I've been a bit of a bitch to Ryan because of his behavior and my hormones.

Maybe it's time I make up for that. I stand before him in my black patent leather thigh high boots, panties, and bra. Ryan sucks his bottom lip between his teeth and rubs his hands together in front of him as he takes me in.

I sway my hips as I walk over to the chaise lounge in our bedroom. The sound of Ryan's growl fills the room. He slaps my ass as he comes up behind me. I look over my shoulder and smile at him.

"You sure you want to play this game with me?" he says and lifts a brow.

Slowly, I take a seat on the lounge, spread my legs and place my forearms on my thighs. I lick my lips before biting down on the bottom one.

"Only one way to find out. Drop your pants and come here, Ry," I purr.

"Look at my baby," he says as he unfastens his belt. "Where'd my innocent girl go?"

I tilt my head to the side. "I don't think you'll be asking for her when I'm done," I say and wink.

Reaching for the remote we keep on this side of the room; I dim the lights and switch to the red ones to set the mood then turn the music on. Arctic Monkey's "Do I Wanna Know?" comes blaring through the speakers.

This will do, I nod my head in satisfaction. I scoot to the edge of my seat and reach for him as he springs free from his pants. Looking up at him through my lashes, I spit on his shaft and work my hand through the moisture.

Ryan

I hiss out a breath as Carmen covers my tip with her mouth. I can't help reaching out and pushing a hand through her hair to watch it slip through my fingers. I fist the strands on the second pass and guide her as she bobs back and forth over my length.

I groan deep in the back of my throat as she hollows her cheeks only to release me from her mouth with a wet slurping sound. I step in closer, guiding my cock back to her mouth.

"Damn, baby, just like that," I grunt when she spits on me again, before sucking the side, as she lifts me toward my stomach and then gobbles me down like her favorite popsicle.

She doesn't stop sucking as she reaches behind her back and unfastens the clasp of her bra. My mouth drops open as her breasts bounce free. The sight of her mounds and the sound of her slurping are a euphoric mix I can't even describe.

I tighten my hold in her hair and step forward until she starts to make that choking sound and pushes at my thighs. I back off, popping free from her mouth as she looks up at me through watery eyes.

However, this doesn't stop her. She pumps me with her hands and flicks her tongue around the crown. Is it clear yet why I love this woman? Her head game is epic and she's the mother of the greatest thing I've done in my life.

The thought of her carrying my second seed turns me on so much I can't take much more of this. I drop to my knees and hike her legs over my shoulders.

She yelps as I hook my fingers in the crotch of her panties and twist, before tearing them from her body. She's already wet as I drag my fingers through her seam. I push two fingers in, and her heat sucks me right in. Then she wants to know why I can't pull out. This is the kind of pussy that makes you forget your name.

"Ry," she whimpers.

"I'm just getting started. You wanted to play, let's play, baby."

I bury my face in her core and she starts to rock her hips greedily in time to the music. I hum into her sweet honey, enjoying the taste on my tongue.

How didn't I realize she's pregnant?

I notice all the changes now as I feast on her and look up at her fuller breasts. I truly hope it's a boy this time. I'm a bit jealous of Noah. Two boys back-to-back.

Although I'll love our baby no matter what we have. It's just sometimes, I wish a had a little guy to roughhouse with. My nephews keep me on my toes, and I can already see the bond the boys all have with each other even at this young age.

I want my boy to be a part of that. It's like watching the seven of us all over again. Carmen's moans bring me back to the present and I concentrate on my task with all my focus.

Her stomach quivers as I push my face in deeper and send my tongue as far as it will go. Placing two fingers on her clit, I then rub until she squirts all over my face.

Palming my face, I begin to drag my hand down to catch the sticky mess. Carmen moans and grabs my hand to bring it to her mouth to lick it clean. I grin and lift a brow.

"Trade places, I want to ride you," she says in this sexy voice that has me so hard my head hurts.

She doesn't have to ask me twice. I pull her up and spin her back to me as I wrap an arm around her waist, then I take her place on the lounge. Carmen straddles my legs and reaches between her legs for my cock.

I hold her hips as she slowly slides down on me. My tongue is pressed against my upper lip as I watch my shit disappear as if her fat ass has swallowed it. She rocks and grinds on me a few times, coating me in her cream. It's an amazing sight.

I slap her ass to watch it bounce and jiggle. She creams some more and groans. She's so damn sexy.

Wanting to see more of her exquisite body, I look into the mirror across the room. It's illuminated by its own light that's triggered when we use the red lights. I bite my lips as my eyes connect with hers.

Carmen gives me a saucy grin and reaches for her breasts to cup them and play with her nipples. I grow harder from the view. She sucks her lip into her mouth and whimpers.

Not able to just watch, I still her hips and drill up into her from beneath. Our groans and moans start to mix as the slapping sound of me getting in her guts fills the air.

"Ry," she gasps as I reach for her clit.

She looks down in awe as she starts to bounce on me again. Her brows knit and her mouth falls open. Suddenly, she starts to shake uncontrollably. I have to wrap my arms around her to keep her upright.

She moves her legs on the inside of mine to close them. After grinding a few times, she throws one leg back over my thigh and plants her heel in the lounge as she reaches for her clit and goes back to ride the shit out of me.

"Fuck, baby," I grunt. Sweat drips down my face and her back.

I use my forearm to wipe the bead of sweat from the tip of my nose. I can tell her legs are getting tired. I'm soaked in her juices, but I'm not ready to be done.

I reach under her legs and lift her to pump up into her again. Then I still and bounce her up and down on my length. The sweet scent of her lotion fills my nostrils as her sweat intensifies the smell.

"Fuck, Ry, yes," she cries out. "I'm going to come, baby. I'm going to come."

"Tell me something I don't know," I growl in her ear as her tight pussy clenches me.

She whimpers and comes. I lock my hand into her hair and tug her head back as I swivel my hips and pound out my own release, I'm getting so deep she's on her toes as if she can get away from me. I love how her legs are shaking and her knees turn in as if she can lock me out.

"Who else can give you this?" I bite out. "All this belongs to you."

She can't even respond, as she quivers and quakes. I lick at the trail of sweat at the center of her back. Her heat squeezes me hard as she screams. I explode, grinning like a fool.

CHAPTER SEVENTEEN

Remember When

Joe

I look through my emails to confirm the schedule for the coming weeks. I need to do some traveling after the holidays to clear some things up for the Alliance. I didn't understand one day I'd be in the middle of all this when my nephew first brought it to me and his father.

Now, I see there was never a way I wouldn't be. From the moment I married Cass, I set so much in motion. Who am I kidding? This was my father's doing all along. He baited generations into this.

I shake my head at my thoughts and toss my phone down on the nightstand. The sound of the bathroom door opening pulls my attention. I turn as Cass turns the lights out.

"I'm tired," she sighs.

"You can sleep in tomorrow."

"Ach, I wish. Paloma wants me to meet her to approve the wedding gown design. She should probably know Carmen is expecting again." She chuckles. "I'm sure whatever Ry stole to get her Carmen's measurements isn't going to do. Do ye know the fool got busted in her closet? She accused him of cross dressing. I could strangle him."

I burst into laughter as I move to climb beneath the sheets. I pull my exhausted wife onto my chest. She looks up at me and smiles sleepily.

"It will all be over soon."

"Will it? We went from a Christmas wedding to Christmas Eve, now where are we?" She snorts.

"New Year's Eve," I reply tiredly, feeling drained just talking about the topic.

"I've threatened to kill him if he changes one more time. I mean it, I do."

I lift her face up with my fingertips under her chin to peck her lips. "I know you do. The staff at the castle can't accommodate another change so New Year's Eve it is. We just have to make it to his big reveal."

"If he doesn't ruin it all before then."

I scoff. "Enough about him. Remember when we married in Scotland? You were so beautiful."

"Aye, and I married the most strapping lad. You know, if I had to do it all again, I'd marry ye again. I'd change nothing."

"Is that right? Not even our wedding night?"

Her checks flush. "No, not even the wedding night. You know, I already knew you were a kinky fucker by then. You only proved me right."

I release a loud laugh. "You loved every minute of it," I say.

"One of me best memories to this day. You know, I think Noah was conceived that night."

I snort. "I know he was."

"I forgot to tell ye, John said he found your stash when he was younger." She shakes her head. "I told you we needed to hide those things better. Those nosey little fuckers used to get into everything."

"The apple doesn't fall far from the tree. They would have turned out the same way no matter what. Are you forgetting what my father gave me for my eighteenth birthday?

"If you ask me, I don't think a single one of our daughters-in-law are complaining about how our sons turned out. Besides, with friends like Nicholas Lincoln, The Club Desire twins, and their uncle Ronan, it was inevitable."

"Aye, ye don't tell a fib."

"Tell me, love. Are you too tired for a little tying up?"

She smiles and reaches to squeeze my growing length. "Well, look at that. I think I found my second wind."

I chuckle and roll to reach into my drawer for the rope and oil. We may not be as young as we used to be, but we still can put those youngins to shame for trying to follow in our footsteps.

When I turn back to my wife. She has already discarded her night gown and sits on her knees in the center of the bed waiting for me. I lick my lips and look over her body. Cass is still as sexy as the night I first saw her wiggling like she needed medical attention.

I grin and turn to put on some Barry White to set the mood before we get started. My smile grows as I remember the times when the music was more to cover the noise we make from a house full of kids. While I love my boys, I'm glad they're gone. We haven't had to use a ball gag in years.

Twenty minutes later when Cass squeals, "Joe." My heart swells. No one can call my name and get my blood flowing like Cass. Tied up, ass pink from my palm, with a look of ecstasy on her face as she drips down my balls, She's the perfect complement to everything I am.

CHAPTER EIGHTEEN

Surprise

Ryan

Luck must be on my side. Carmen has been too distracted by morning sickness to notice too much this morning. Things like the "Loaner car" we're in. It's not a loaner at all. It's her first Christmas gift.

"Which car did you say went in for service? We don't have a Mercedes." I feel my face drain of blood. Maybe I'm not so lucky.

I tap my fingers against the steering wheel and look into the rearview mirror. Don't ask me what I'm looking for. I peek out the corner of my eye at Carmen and suck in a calming breath.

"You're acting weird again," she grumbles from her seat beside me.

She pops me in the shoulder, then pouts and folds her arms across her chest. I know I am. Today's the day I reveal what I've been up to and in a week she will have the wedding of her dreams… I hope.

I still don't know if I got this right. I'm so nervous my stomach is bubbling.

She has mentioned this GLC 300 on multiple occasions. However, as we stepped from the house to load up the car with gifts, she asked if this one came in Black. I got her the white one.

I groan, I'm already fucking this up. A year of planning and it's all going to shit. *Come on, Ry, get it together.*

It's Christmas day and the family is gathering at Mom and Dad's. The plan is for everyone to open their gifts. When Carmen's opens hers, it will be the key to the truck and a wedding planning book I had custom made for her with pictures of the castle and a message in the back.

I try to calm myself down. When I peek over at her, it's clear she's getting agitated by the second. That's not good for the baby, I try to think fast to get her to relax.

I lick my lips. "I have something on my mind," I murmur.

"If this is about this gift you've been working on. I'll be so glad when you give it to me."

I glance away from the rode quickly to wink at her and bite my lip. "Oh, I'm going to give it to you all right."

A pretty blush comes to her checks as she looks back at me. She scoffs, her eyes glazing over as if she's in a distant memory. After squirming in her seat, she rolls her eyes. However, a small smile plays at the corner of her lips.

I spent this morning with my face buried between her thighs to calm my anxiety. She's probably remembering that.

Good, she's distracted from my weirdo behavior.

I stop at a light and shoot a text to Mom to see if everyone else is there. Carmen's eyes are on me, watching my every move. I pull off as the light changes and turn into Mom and Dad's neighborhood. It's not that far from our place.

My phone goes off with a text. I pull in behind Noah's Hummer and look down at my phone. I snort at the text.

Mom: *Don't be asking me who's in my home. Just get your ass here.*

"Oh, Ry, before I forget. Can you watch Jordan tomorrow? I need to get some editing done on my short," Carmen says as she turns to look at me.

I think I break out into a sweat. I run a hand through my hair. I've gotten this far and it's going to blow up in my face. She's supposed to start a week of pampering tomorrow before we board our flight to Scotland.

"Fuck," I huff.

Jordan gasps in the back from her car seat. "Daddy, no," she chastises me. "Bad word. Don't say that."

I roll my eyes as Carmen laughs. "What's the big deal? You'll be home with us anyway. I just need you to keep an eye on her while I concentrate."

"No, no, it's fine."

Cassie

I look out of the window to see Ry and Carmen still in the car. I groan and roll my eyes. I release the curtain and pray for calm.

"Joe, Joe, please get out there and save the lad before he fucks this up," I call out.

The boys in the house chuckle. I roll my eyes. I can't count on them to help. I know the fuckers have a bet going on for when Ry will slip up and ruin all his plans.

"I'll put ants in all ye pants if he screws this up because of one of ye, bunch of melters." I point to Brax. "Shut your bake. I don't want to hear what ye have to say."

He pokes his lip out like the brat he is as I cutoff whatever smart shit was about to come out of his mouth. Heather comes along and hands him the baby and that seems to appease him. The brat.

Joe comes from upstairs and heads out the front door. I pull the curtain back to watch as he walks to the car and pulls Jordan from the backseat, tickling and nuzzling her neck to make her laugh.

Carmen steps from the car before a flustered looking Ryan. I swear, if the lad would have texted me one more time, I was going to ruin it all myself. I've had to call on the patience of baby Jesus waiting on the wise men for this one.

"You have to admit. This is all kinds of romantic," Kaye says. "You can write it in a book."

"Trust me, she has notes," Felix replies.

The lass ducks her head. I'm proud of her and everything she writes. However, I did notice her last two books seemed like romance action movies based on our family. Felix may have to have a talk with her before Joe and I do. Not everything we do should be in a book.

"Come, Toby, lets help them with their gifts," Kamara says.

"We'll take care of that," John croons, tapping Wyatt and Noah on the shoulders as he heads for the door.

"Don't ye three ruin this for him," I hiss.

The bums all snicker at me. I'll kill them meself and help Ry hide the bodies. My poor baby. He's trying so hard to do this for Carmen and as crazy as he made me in the last year, I still want this for him.

"Relax, it's going to be fine," Nellie says as she comes to peek out of the window with me.

I grunt. "Have ye met my youngest child? The overgrown baby jokes so much, he doesn't know how to handle anything serious. He's going to screw this up. I have two grand on it meself."

Nellie gasps then giggles. "No, you didn't?"

"Aye, I did. Got Joe to get in on the boys bet when I found out." I wink. "I intend to make back every dime I spent on all ye wee brats this Christmas."

She cracks up as she shakes her head. A commotion outside grabs our attention. I turn to see Joe slap Wyatt upside the back of his head as Ry looks like his world is about to crumble. Carmen stands looking down at the ground, and that's when I see the open gift box at Ry's feet.

"Uh-oh," Nellie murmurs beside me.

"For Fuck's sake."

Ryan

I stare down at Carmen's Christmas gift, holding my breath. One minute, I had it in my hands trying to tug it away from Wyatt, the next in slow motion it flew up in the air and dropped down to the ground. The lid flew off and the tissue paper and items inside scattered on the ground, revealing all of the contents.

"Hurry up and pick it up," Noah hisses while elbowing me.

I look up at him and the grimace he's giving me. My gaze sweeps over to Carmen. John has her distracted. I don't believe she's seen anything yet. Nellie and Bean rush from the house and grab Carmen's attention and usher her away.

I finally breathe and bend to gather the items and place them back into the box. Wyatt stoops down to help. I can't help glaring at him. He looks at me and frowns.

"Dude, I'm sorry. I was trying to help," he murmurs.

"I told you I had this one."

"Yeah, well, your hands were full, and Jordan was whining for you."

I sigh. "It's fine, she didn't see anything." I dust off the book and place it back into the box with the tissue paper. "Wait, where's the key?"

I know I put the other key to the truck into the box. I kept the spare to drive, but I threaded a thin string through the key to make a little bow and placed it in the box.

"Fuck, Wyatt, you can be such a dick."

"Calm your ass down," he snaps. "There… it's under the truck. Reach one of those long ass arms under there and get it."

"All of you calm down," Daddy hisses.

I look up and Jordan's in his arms, shaking her head as she covers her ears. I groan as I replay in my head my conversation with Wyatt.

There's nothing I can do now. Besides, I'm that little girl's father. She's not the parent. I ignore my daughter's aversion to what she calls bad words and turn my focus back to the key underneath the car.

Yeah, my arms are long, but not long enough to reach the key where it lies. Damn, I'm going to have to move the car to get to it.

"Move out of the way," Noah calls as he goes to get into the driver's seat. "I'll move it, you get the key."

"No, no, no," I call out. "I'm supposed to be the only one who has driven it before her," I growl.

"Are you kidding me?" John and Noah say simultaneously.

"No, I'll move it. One of you get the key."

They roll their eyes. However, John comes and snatches the gift box off the ground. Dad says something in Jordan's ear that makes her laugh and cup his face. I move past them and climb into the car. Dad grabs a few gift bags still in the trunk and moves toward the house.

I back the car up enough to reveal the key beneath. Wyatt scoops it up and dangles it in the air. I narrow my eyes at him and pull back into the spot, causing him to rush out of the way.

I hop out of the truck and move to John's side. Wyatt drops the key into the gift box John is holding. I snatch the box and replace the lid.

Noah places his hands on my shoulders and puts his forehead to mine. "Listen, you have to calm down. You did great. The truck is the cherry on top. I watched the live chat Mom did of the location this morning.

"Connie and the others are coming through for you. It looks awesome. We're all proud of you. Now breathe and get your ass in there so we can all be over this," he says.

Carmen

I don't like the idea of everyone opening gifts one by one. For one, I have to go the bathroom every five seconds and I missed half of the openings. Secondly, my daughter is becoming agitated waiting for her turn.

This little spoiled brat is going to make me pluck her. There are so many of us, it seems like this is taking all day. I look to Ryan and he almost looks green as he clutches Evan in his lap as if the kid is an anchor.

"Please, Jordan and Carmen next," Ryan says when Toby's family finishes opening their gifts.

"All right, all right," Brax murmurs as he puts down the gift, we brought for him. Allowing us to go next.

Ryan and John disappear from the room and return with a huge box with a bow on it. We didn't bring this one in the car. I look at Ry curiously. They set the box down in front of Jordan.

"And this is why she's spoiled. What is that?" I give Ry side eye.

"Just wait, y'all see." He smiles proudly and puffs out his chest.

I release Jordan as she toddles over to the box looking around it as if she has to inspect it first. She looks back at me, then up at her father as if checking for permission.

"Go on, open it. It's yours," Ryan encourages.

She claps her little chubby hands as her face lights up. Ryan squats and ushers her between his legs so he can assist her to peel back the first piece of paper. He makes a ripping sound with his mouth, making Jordan squeal and laugh as she holds the piece of paper in her hand.

Brodie runs over and snatches a large piece off before Noah can snatch him up and chide him. Jordan frowns and throws her body against the gift as if to protect it.

"No, Bro-die. Mine," she scolds.

"You tell him, Jordie," Brax croons.

"These hands," Jordan fusses and shakes her little fist at Brodie.

"Oh my God, did she just threaten for him to catch these hands?" Heather gasps and cracks up.

"Yeah, she did, and your husband is the one who taught her that," Ryan says and rolls his eyes.

Jordan rocks her jaw and rolls her eyes. Ryan reaches for her and pulls her from the box. "Come on, baby. Let's get the rest off. Everyone's waiting."

She looks at her father and takes a calming breath. I swear, I love this kid, but I don't know where I got her from. She's like an old woman in a baby's body.

He helps our little girl to tear the rest of the wrapping paper off the box. Wyatt and Ry work together to help Jordan take the lid off the box.

My mouth pops open. "Really, Ryan?"

"What?" he says as Jordan squeals and tries to get into the custom-made Bentley coup power wheel.

"I know you spent a ton on that thing. She's barely four yet."

He scowls. "And when she's four, I'll upgrade her. We'll be able to control this one for her. It's perfectly safe."

I look at the smile on my baby's face and I don't have it in me to argue. I can't help smiling as wide as she is. Ryan is such a good father, Jordan adores him. I know he'll be awesome to the new baby.

"Now, it's your turn," Ryan says as he places a box in my lap and leans in to whisper close to my ear before brushing my hair aside with his nose and planting a kiss behind my ear.

I look down at the box he's been so protective of all day. It's the one Wyatt dropped. I couldn't make out what had spilled from it before Nellie and Bean came to drag me into the house.

I look up into his eyes and he pecks my lips. Excitement explodes within. I'll finally get to know what he's been up to that has caused him to act like a weirdo for months.

I cheese like a lunatic as I pull the top off the box and push the tissue paper aside. My shoulders slump and I knit my brows in confusion as I look down at the white photo album looking book and key resting on top. None of this explains his behavior.

I reach for the key with the bow on it first. I look up at Ry to find his face a little crestfallen. I tilt my head to the side.

"Babe?" I'm a little confused myself. Ryan just bought me a Bentley last year. Jordan's power wheel looks exactly like it.

I look back to the key and it clicks. The truck outside, the one he drove us over in, its mine. I gasp.

"You got me the GLC," I say excitedly.

"You said you wanted it. We can change the color if you like."

"No, no, babe. It's perfect, but what's with the book? And why would you be in my closet for a car?"

"Open the book. You'll see."

I eye him suspiciously and reach to pull the book out, then place it on my lap. It's a pretty album. A pretty lace surrounds it and it's covered in little crystals. A picture from our wedding at the courthouse is on the front.

My heart aches for a moment. I wanted to do things differently. I've watched all my brothers and sisters-in-law have beautiful weddings. The only wedding I didn't get to attend was Wyatt and Nellie's, but from the pictures I've seen, they had a gorgeous wedding as well.

I've felt like I was robbed. Ryan takes a seat beside me as if I'm taking too long. He reaches to open the cover.

"I'm still confused," I whisper as I see the first page in the book. It's a picture of what looks like a castle with rolling hills behind it.

"Keep going," Ryan says nervously.

I shrug and keep turning. My confusion grows. This is like a wedding planner. Pictures of floral arrangements, décor, bridesmaid gowns, tuxes, and a gorgeous horse drawn carriage. I get to the last two pages and tears start to spill as I realize what this gift is. There's a gorgeous wedding invitation and a message.

Our wedding is printed in beautiful lettering on the last page. My lashes are wet as I read beneath these words.

Will you marry me... again?

Ryan groans. "You hate it. I got it wrong, didn't I?"

I slide the book into the gift box before I turn to wrap my arms around his neck. "I love it. Yes, I'll marry you again," I say against he's lips.

"Thank fuck." Cass sighs as if in relief. "Now go on and explain what's going on, Ry, so I can stop clenching me butt cheeks."

"Right," Ry chuckles breathlessly. "We're all flying to Scotland. We're getting married in the family castle. Tomorrow your mom's going to take you for your final dress fitting. She oversaw the design of your gown. That's why I was in your closet. She needed something of yours for the designer to work with.

"The wedding will be on New Year's Eve. I've taken care of everything. It's your dream wedding." He pauses and rubs the back of his neck. "At least, I hope it is. God, is it suddenly hot in here. My stomach hurts."

I squeal as his words sink in and kiss all over his face. I love this man so much. It all makes sense now. And to think I accused him of cheating. Everyone seems to be in on this.

"You all knew?" I choke out as I look around.

Everyone smiles back at me as they nod. Ryan wipes the sweat from his forehead before he rushes from the room. I go to stand and follow to check on him.

"I've got it," Cass says as she follows Ry out. "I want me money," she calls over her shoulder.

John and Noah laugh. "I knew we shouldn't have taken that last bet. Mom set us up." John chuckles.

I tune them all out as I flip through my gift again. If these are all the things Ry has planned for the wedding, it's going to be gorgeous. I'm so excited and can't wait. The castle is breathtaking.

Nellie and Bean come to sit beside me. "I'm getting my dream wedding," I gush.

"He has been so nervous. He worked really hard to put this all together. He's been driving everyone crazy." Nellie frowns, then laughs.

"I don't think everyone will get any sleep until the wedding is over. He's like a bridezilla," Roni says from across the room.

"I think it's cute," Kamara says as Toby takes the baby from her. They were so happy to have another little boy.

I place a hand over my still flat tummy. A baby, a wedding and a man I couldn't love more. This is life. The best Christmas ever.

CHAPTER NINETEEN

Sneak Away

Cassie

I stand in the threshold of our living room watching our grands and children. Ryan has finally settled after I made him a cup of tea for his nervous stomach. Carmen hasn't stopped looking at him like he's a star in the sky that has learned to speak.

We've spent the entire day opening gifts and watching the kids have fun with their new toys. Those little troublemakers have found their way into everything they can.

Riley and Jordan found their way into my study and tried to climb the bookshelves. If Joe and I hadn't been trying to sneak away one of them could have gotten hurt. Bad enough Jordan fell when Joe's voice boomed through the room. You would have thought she'd seen a ghost.

I'm still shaken up, even though she only fell from the third shelf and onto her bottom. The little stinker only pouted after she got over the shock of falling.

The familiar feel of heavy arms resting on my waist causes me to look up over my shoulder. Joe's eyes sparkle as he looks down at me. This man is just as handsome as the day I met him.

"Everyone has opened their gifts except for you. You've been seeing to everyone else," he says smoothly.

I lift a brow. "Gift, what gift?"

He lifts his hand with a rectangle shaped gift box with a tiny gold bow on it in his palm. I take the box and open it.

I gasp and tears come to my eyes. It's a gorgeous bracelet made of three connected rings. I pull the bracelet out to get a closer look.

"Joe, its beautiful."

"The rings represent the generations. We're on the inside ring. The second ring has the birthstones of the boys and the girls. The third ring holds the birthstones of the grands."

I watch as the gemstones slide around the rings as I examine them. I tilt it in the opposite direction and they slide back. I notice the boys' stones are next to the birthstones of their wives. It's breathtaking to see our family together like this.

"I had it made so we can always add to it. As the family keeps growing."

I launch myself at Joe. He catches me and holds me tight. This is such a thoughtful gift. I kiss him and hold his face to mine.

"What say ye? We can go upstairs and finish what we started this morning before Toby and his monsters interrupted," I purr.

"I've been trying to get my hands on you all day. We should send them all home now. They've been fed, we've given out all the gifts." Joe frowns, but his eyes twinkle with mischief.

"If it wasn't Christmas, I'd have thrown them out hours ago. Let the wee ones have their fun with their cousins. We can just sneak away for a bit."

"Okay, fine." He looks over my head. "Quick, it looks like their all down here. We can go up to my mancave. They won't let the kids on the steps."

"If any of their grown asses finds us, they'll get what they deserve. It's not like they all haven't fucked all around our house as it is."

Joe chuckles and shoves me gently toward the stairs. TJ runs over as we're about a foot away from the steps. He has a wide smile on his face. "Grandpa Joe look what I got," TJ calls.

Joe palms the top of his head and turns him around. "Not now, son. You can show Grandpa whatever it is in an hour or two. Go find something to do until I get back."

I roll my lips to keep from laughing. Joe swats my butt as he follows me up the stairs. Anticipation fills me, almost thirty-five years and this man still makes my entire body hum. Once at the top of the stairs. I turn for Joe's mancave.

We scurry inside before we're stopped again. Almost everyone knows not to come in here uninvited. Once inside, Joe closes the door behind us.

I stop next to his recliner and stand with my back to him. This is an old dance I know well. Joe primed me to his liking from the start of our marriage.

I know my man and what pleases him. Joe has never tried to change me outside of the bedroom and in return, I've been everything he wants and demands inside. I believe it's made our love stronger.

Joe comes up behind me and cups my breasts over my dress, kneading them. I almost burst from his touch. I've been waiting all day. I've been high off emotions and my body is buzzing with the extra energy that has transformed into lust and desire for my husband.

"Should we do this fast and simple or are you in the mood for rough, dirty, and a few hours?" he whispers in my ear.

I look over my shoulder and wiggle my ass into him. "Ye already know the answer to that."

He dips his head and captures my lips as he kneads my mounds and pinches my nipples. The sweet pain of his rough, large fingers causes me to whimper into his mouth.

He bites my lip as he smiles against my mouth. "Take off your clothes."

He doesn't have to tell me twice. I wiggle out of my dress quickly and peel out of my bra and panties. Joe rushes forward in all his naked glory and lifts me onto his waist. He brushes hungry kisses across my breasts and collarbone. I can't keep my hands from roaming his smooth skin and strong shoulders.

I'm dripping wet for him, and he's barely touched me yet. I cry out when he wraps a hand around my neck and traps one of my nipples in his warm mouth. I'm lightheaded from the contact, missing the fact he moves us to his recliner.

I yelp a little as the cool leather meets my overheated skin. With his hand still firmly around my neck, he starts to kiss his way down my body. He releases my throat and moves away briefly, allowing me to catch my breath for a moment.

I blink at the ceiling, bracing myself for what's to come. "Get into position," Joe commands.

I don't hesitate to draw my legs into my chest and hold onto the backs of my thighs. I bring my eyes down to his and find intense desire staring back at me. His thick erection points straight up toward his six pack that still looks as firm as the first time I saw him naked, if not more so.

He slips a towel beneath me before he starts to pour oil onto my breasts and down my center. I can't help laughing. This isn't the first time we've done this in this room. I'm sure he has more than oil in here.

"You're still as gorgeous as the first time I saw you," he says gruffly.

"I was thinking the same thing," I reply.

My words turn into moans as he lowers and places his hands over mine, holding onto the backs of my thighs. His warm mouth does all the talking we need. Joe takes care with eating pussy as if he doesn't want to miss a spot.

In all these years, I've never been disappointed. Each time is better than the last. He has mastered my body and I have no problem following his lead to my pleasure.

"Mmm," he hums into me.

"Yes, Joe, yes."

He grunts and lifts, before pulling my bottom to the edge of the chair. I watch with my mouth open as he palms his cock and guides himself into me. He covers my mouth with his hand, and pounds deeply into me hard.

He snaps and rolls his hips like he's on the dance floor, then pounds into me with long strokes. I cry into his hand as my sex soaks him, begging for more with each wet pass.

I start to clench my walls around him, and he groans and grunts. My scalp begins to tingle, and I curl my toes. I'm stuffed like a Thanksgiving bird and happily willing to take more.

He slaps my ass. "You like that, love. Your pussy is so wet." He lifts to plant his feet on the floor, lifting one foot onto the arm of the recliner and thrusts down into me.

I throw my head back, almost breaking the seal of his hand over my mouth. My cries slip free, but I could care less. My eyes rolls back as he pauses to allow his length to pulse within me before grinding hips and balls against me, pushing in as deep as he can go at this angle.

Nellie

"Anyone see Mom?" Brax asks.

I look around. I haven't seen Joe or Cass in like about an hour. As I make the realization, everyone else confirms they haven't either. I shrug and get up to go to the restroom. When I get to the first-floor powder room it's occupied.

"Ugh," I huff, this is the only downside to having such a large family.

I groan and head upstairs to use one of the bathrooms up there. I handle my business and wash my hands. When I go to head back downstairs, noise from Joe's mancave catches my attention. I head that way, hoping one of the kids didn't sneak up here to mess with Joe's things.

When I get to the door the sounds get louder. I pull a face because it sounds a lot like someone's watching porn in there. I think about the stories I've heard the guys tell about their start with watching dirty movies and my mind turns to Dae-Dae and TJ. I can't remember if I saw them amongst the kids downstairs.

Everyone's attention had been on my son and Noah's boys. I purse my lips wanting to laugh. It's not funny, but it sort of is.

Evan and Brodie tried to put Connor in the washing machine and wash him after he spilled eggnog on his shirt.

You have to keep an eye on these kids. I turn the knob and peak my head into the room then freeze. I know I should back out and close the door, but I can't. I tilt my head to the side and blink a few times to make sure I'm seeing what my brain tells me I am.

Joe's pounding Cass out from behind like he's a twenty-year-old. She's on her knees in his recliner as he stands behind her. He slaps her ass, turning it red then pulls out and rubs between her legs as she squirts.

"Ah fuck, Joe."

He swiftly slams back into her, then lifts her leg out to the side to hold it up as he drives into her. Cass squeals a little and that's when I realize Joe's covering her mouth to cover her cries. Not that it's helping a whole lot.

He lifts on his toes as he gets more into it. His calves flex with the force of his thrusts. His grunts becoming louder.

I should back away. I know I should, but my feet feel like they're in quicksand. I'm trapped in awe. Unable to process how these two are doing this and making it look so effortless.

Their harsh breathing reaches me by the door, yet I still can't look away. Sweat drips down Joe's back into the crack of his ass. How? How does this sixty-year-old man look like this? I'm dumbfounded.

Do Wy and I look this good having sex? These two are mesmerizing. Simply beautiful. Joe places his hand on his lower back as he thrusts forward, leaving Cass's moans to fill the room. His other hand is pressed to the center of her back, holding her in place as he pumps roughly inside her.

"Fuck, yes, Joe. Just like that. Harder, harder, I'm coming."

He slaps her ass again. “Always telling me something I already know. You think I can’t feel what I’m doing to your pussy? Come for me, love. I’m waiting.”

I shove my fist into my mouth. This is insane. Shit, that’s hot. Will this be me and Wyatt in thirty years? I hope so.

Joe pulls out of Cass as she sprays all over the place. I swear I want to fist pump the air. I’m so proud of them. My father-in-law just slayed the pussy like a porn star champ and my mother-in-law took that dick down like a fucking pro and they’re both over fifty.

It’s when Cass hops up and drops to her knees, grabbing his still hard dick and wraps her lips around it as Joe scoops up her hair, I finally snap out of it. I gasp and stumble back. They both snap their heads in my direction.

I cover my eyes and back out of the room. I take off as fast as I can to get as far away as I can. I cover my eyes like I should have done from the start and race down the stairs blindly. I stumble and have to catch myself on the railing. I have to take a seat before I rise and start racing down again.

“Oh my God, Oh my God,” I cry out as I go.

Cassie

“Shit, Joe. Ye didn’t lock the door?”

I look up at my red-faced husband as he finds a towel to clean us up and starts to gather our clothes for us to dress. I purse my lips as I see my job isn’t finished. I had planned to suck the life from Joe after that gift he just gave me. I’m still throbbing between the legs for him.

"I… I thought I did," he says. "How much do you think she saw?" he says as his cheeks turn brighter with embarrassment.

"Oh, Joe please, we paid for this house years ago. It's ye and me name on this deed. Who's going to check me in me own damn home? I'm fifty-five and can still give my husband a proper shagging. As I should. Come, I have a few words for that lass," I say as I fix my clothes.

CHAPTER TWENTY

Jingle Bells

Wyatt

"Oh my God, oh my god, oh my God," Nellie chants repeatedly as she rushes down the stairs in my parent's home.

I stand up with Evan in my arms. His little ass needed a time out. I swear, if there's trouble my son and Brodie are in the middle of it. I place Evan on his feet and of course he takes off across the room for his Uncle Ry.

Ryan and Brax are going to pay for the shit they're teaching my son. I hope they have all girls, seven of them each. With the pretty as sin girls we've been making in this family, it would serve them right.

Nora is five and those golden eyes and thick, long lashes have boys handing over their candy. Lulu had a wedding in school during recess. Toby's been talking about home schooling since. Yup, I hope Ryan and Brax have nothing but girls.

I narrow my eyes at my son as he wiggles up under his Uncle and looks back at me warily. My hand has a meeting with his little ass later. How do two four-year olds get a three-year old, that's damn near just as big as them, inside the washing machine. Brodie and Evan were literally trying to wash Connor.

Noah found them just in time. Brodie is still sniffling in the corner. Noah loves his boys, but he's serious with his discipline. Bean has been pouting because Noah won't let her cuddle Brodie after having his little butt tanned.

Connor, the poor little guy, doesn't know any better. He's been right under Brodie, trying to share his cookies with him, to make him feel better. I love these kids.

Speaking of love. I turn back to my wife with concern. Her checks are purple, and she looks like she's seen a ghost.

"What's wrong?" I ask as I move toward her.

"I… I didn't mean to watch. I… I was in shock. I mean, they're so old and… I didn't think… Oh, My God. I don't think I snapped out of it until she dropped to her knees." Nellie pinches her eyes closed and gulps. "What the hell did I just watch?"

Brax bursts into laughter. "Sounds like she caught Mom and Dad going at it again," he barks out through his laughter.

I bite my lip, trying not to laugh at my wife when her cheeks darken some more. Fucking adorable. Her eyes are so big and round behind her glasses. My brothers and I find this hilarious. I think I'm the only one still holding on.

"You guys, this is not funny," she hisses in embarrassment.

"What, you think you're the first to catch them?" Ryan snorts.

"Fuck, I asked Dad for some pointers after the shit I saw," Brax cracks up.

Jordan gasps in his lap and looks up at him. "No, bad words, Bra-Brac," she scowls at him, sending us all into more fits of laughter.

This time I can't hold mine in. I wrap an arm around my blushing wife and pull her into my chest. I kiss the top of her head as she shakes it.

Braxton pretends to gobble up the little finger Jordan points at him. "Your Uncle Brax is so sorry, Princess," Brax coos at Jordan.

She shakes her head at him like she's so disappointed and climbs off his lap. I watch in amusement as her little chubby legs carry her over to her mother. I swear, I don't know how that kid became the swearing police. Her father curses like a sailor and she's around Mom more than any of the other kids.

Jordan settles in her mother's lap with her arms crossed over her little chest, while she looks over at Brax with the evil eye. Just then, my mother storms into the room with my crimson faced father following behind her.

I roar with laughter as Dad will look anywhere but at my wife. At least one of them has the nerve to be embarrassed. Mom… never going to happen.

"Nellie Black, I want ye to know I've been polishing his knob for longer than ye all have been alive." Mom tosses her thumb over her shoulder, pointing to Dad. "It's kept his cock at home, where it belongs. This is my home, for fuck's sake and I will not apologize for it.

"I've caught you in my home with Wyatt between yer thighs more times than I can count. Get over it or get out," Mom huffs and folds her arms over her chest.

"Oh My God," all the wives and girlfriends say in unison as they all cover their faces.

I immediately look at Jordan. She has her ears covered with her tiny hands as she shakes her head and scowls at Mom. My stomach hurts I'm laughing so hard.

Nellie pulls out of my arms and starts to collect our things. I fold my arms over my chest as I watch her. Out of the corner of my eye, I catch Heather biting her fist to keep from laughing. Bean wipes tears from her eyes as her shoulders shake.

"Lass, what the hell are ye doing?" My mother says with her hands on her hips.

"You just told me to leave." Nellie blinks at my mother.

My mother rolls her eyes. "Nellie, ye saw a little cock in my mouth, get over it." My mother waves her off.

"Oh, God, I saw more than a *little* cock and way more than it in your mouth." Nellie collapses in the seat next to her. "God, Wy, you better be able to do shit like that when we're old."

"Who are ye calling old?" Mom snaps. "How exactly do you think we made seven boys?"

Then something I have seen few times in my going on thirty-five years of life happens. Dad growls and storms over to Mom. He grabs her by the waist and lifts her until they're at eye level. Then he kisses her into silence and submission.

When he breaks the kiss, Mom actually blushes. She places her face in his neck, in an uncharacteristic show of shyness. Dad surprises me again when he turns with Mom in his arms and starts back for upstairs.

"Show yerselves and yer bad ass children out. Merry Christmas and good night," Daddy calls over his shoulder. His Scottish brogue comes to the surface, telling me he means business.

"I guess they weren't finished," Heather howls out in laughter.

CHAPTER TWENTY-ONE

Our Beginning

Cassie

A week later (The night before the wedding) …

We arrived in Scotland this morning. Memories of my wedding have been playing in my mind all day. I couldn't be happier for Ryan, the staff here at the castle has done a spectacular job.

The cherry blossoms look so whimsical in this grand hall. The lighting has given the place an ethereal presence. I haven't been able to leave out of this breathtaking room since I came to check in. I run my hand over one of the crisp table clothes.

My hearts squeezes and I reach up to sweep at a tear. Papa Black would have been so proud of these lads. He loved those boys so and treated me like a daughter. It hurt as much as if I had lost me own father when he passed.

When we arrived today, we were welcomed to the castle like royals. I almost forgot how grand this place is. It took my breath away the first time Joe brought me here. I understood from the time we arrived on his father's doorstep why my da choose Joe for me.

The Black clan came with its own perks. The Blacks are the closest I could get to royalty without me actually marrying into a royal family like Toby did. No wonder he found himself a princess.

"Hey, Aunt Cass," Logan's voice pulls me from my musing.

I turn with a wide smile. This lad has grown to be one strapping man. A green-eyed version of me boys. Less happy than he used to be as a boy and young man, but still easy on the eyes.

"Logan, it's good to see ye. Thank ye so much for doing this for Ryan."

"No problem at all, Aunt Cassie. Grandda would have wanted it this way. He didn't just leave the place for me. He left it for the family. Ya all be welcome anytime ya need."

I reach to pat his arm. "How's yer wee one? Where is she?"

He sucks in a deep breath. "She's still breathing, I haven't killed her by accident. Her hair might be a mess, but she's clean and fed," he says with a sheepish look on his face. "She ran into the other kids and took off."

"Ye still chasing those sassy knickers?"

"She doesn't wear knickers, Aunt Cass," he says with a wink. "Besides, I do believe it was your husband who taught me never chase what's already mine."

I laugh and shake my head. "Well, ye be careful. I'm going to finish me walk through and make sure everything is up to Ryan's standards." I roll my eyes.

Logan leans in and kisses my cheek. The boy smells nice. I don't think that lass has much of a shot getting away from him. Me nephews are as determined as me boys. I wish them all happiness.

When Logan steps away, I catch sight of Connie, Brooklyn, and Dylan. I give them a quick wave as I head for the gardens where the ceremony will take place. They're putting the last of the cherry blossoms in place.

The sunlight hits the altar in just the right way. I know this will all be stunning tomorrow. Carmen is one lucky girl.

I remember Joe having this place decked out for me. He had to plan everything since I'd never been here before and I was so pregnant with Wyatt during the planning. I gave input as much as I could but Joe did most of the work and it was a day I will never forget.

However, it's our wedding night that's still burned into my brain. It was when I learned how kinky my husband could be. It was more than the positions he'd placed me in starting from that first night in Ireland.

Joe guided me into his tastes and pleasures. I remember being so young and innocent. I had no idea what I'd gotten myself into. All I knew was I loved him and was willing to do just about anything he asked.

"Where are we going?" I asked as my new husband led me away from the bedroom I was told would be ours during our stay.

We were both only dressed in black silk robes. After I bathed and rubbed oil into my skin, Joe wrapped me in this robe and led me from the room. The halls of the castle are chilly so I hurry my steps to keep up with Joe's long strides.

Me mother had taken Wyatt for the night so my husband and I could have some alone time. I started to become nervous as we moved through the castle. What if they needed to find us if something happened with the baby and we aren't in our room?

"Trust me, love. I want to share something with you," Joe said and gave my hand a gentle squeeze.

I made myself relax. He had done nothing but protect me and our son since I showed up on his doorstep. I'd fallen madly in love with him and couldn't wait to see what the rest of our lives would be like.

He came to a stop in front of double doors and smiled at me. I lifted a brow, eyeing him suspiciously. "What are ya up to, Joe Black?" I asked.

"I want to see how far I can push your limits. It's time you learn more about me in the bedroom. I believe we have something special we can explore. If you don't want to try, say the word. We can turn around now and go back to our rough vanilla sex. However, I get the feeling you'll be into adding a little spice to our fucking. Something tells me you're the perfect wife and submissive for me."

"I don't know about this submissive business, me father didn't hand ya a slave, but I'm not opposed to a little spicy," I said and bit my lips.

"Oh, love, it's about more than you being my sex slave. The power I will hand to you will make you more fierce than you already are. In reality, I'm the slave to your pleasure and care. I will teach you to trust me in every aspect of our lives as I push you to heights you've yet to know."

"Why are ya still talking? Is it a Scottish thing?"

Joe roars with laughter before backing me into the door to crowd my space, grabbing the back of my neck, and crushing my lips with his. His kiss was possessive and demanding. It was in that moment, I knew I was in for something I hadn't known up until that point.

Joe changed right before my eyes. He lifted his free hand to grasp my throat and dropped his other hand from the back of my neck to my arse. I wrapped my hand around his wrist clutching my throat, lifting on my toes to try to get closer to him.

Joe nipped and sucked at my lips, teasing and taunting me. He consumed my senses so of course I didn't notice him open the door behind me. I followed his led as he sipped and drank from my mouth. When he pulled away, he had a huge smile on his face.

I turned to look around the room and gasped. "What is this?"

"It's called a playroom. My father gifted it to me when I turned eighteen."

I turn to look up at him with a lifted brow. The only things in here that resemble a playroom are the adult swing suspended from the ceiling and maybe the soft pallet of pillows that seem to make a bed area off to the right.

Other than that there's some type of huge wheel in the center of the room, a cross in the corner of the left side, a bed that anchors the room, and a throne with restraints at the foot from what I can see. There are some other furnishings as well. However, what's most interesting are the walls lined with shelves showcasing all kinds of kinky looking fuckery.

"Aren't ya a wee bit old for playing?" I tease when I finally find my words.

"Ask me that again when we're done. This will get as intense as you can stand. Which means you need to pick a safe word that will let me know you're at your limit. You're only to use it if you truly can't take or don't want anymore."

"America." It pops off my lips as soon as he finishes his words.

He chuckles and nods as he reaches for my robe and releases the tie. I watch as his eyes seem to transform with desire. It had only been a little over a month since I had Wyatt, I was a little self-conscious at first.

As if reading my thoughts, Joe moved swiftly. Grabbing the back of my neck to spin me into his chest. My back to his front. It happens so fast, my chest heaves as I startle.

He leans into my ear and cups my sex. "You're gorgeous. My son came from this sexy body. Everything about you is perfect for me, Cass. Never doubt yourself. You're a Black now. You will teach our children to be confident in everything they do, which means from this day forward you hold your head up and represent our family the same," he says all this while making circles around my clit.

I lift on my toes as he pushes two fingers into me. He moves his lips to suck at the skin on my neck. I'm breathless as I try to ride out the wave of pleasure.

He slaps my mound before he shoves his fingers back inside. "Say, yes, sir. I want to hear you understand me."

I looked up at him in awe. Not of him, but of me because I plan to obey his command. How did I get to this point? Joe only smiled knowingly.

"Yes, sir. I understand."

And that was the start. Joe moved me through his entire playroom teaching me to play his way.

I come back from the memory as my husband walks up behind me, placing his strong arms around my waist. His scent engulfs me. For thirty-five years, I've known safety in this man's arms.

That night he hung me upside down in a swing I didn't think would hold me, but he was more than enough support even if the swing had given while he took possession of my body.

He nuzzles my neck. "What are you thinking about?"

"Our wedding and wedding night," I say with a wide smile.

He chuckles. "I still have the key to the playroom. Maybe we should visit."

"Why did we never make one in the house? Sneaking into clubs has gotten harder with age."

"You were the one who said you didn't want one in the house with the boys. They're all gone now, we can have a contractor in as soon as we get back home."

I smile and turn in his arms. "Yeah, it may be time. I almost blew that young lass's head off last time for eyeing you in your leather chaps."

He roars with laughter. "I only have eyes for you. Come on, Paloma's looking for you. They're setting up the dining hall for the rehearsal dinner."

"I saw Logan and a few others. Are they the only ones to arrive?"

"No, it looks like New York has arrived together. I saw Uri and LaSalle heading for the bar with Cole."

"Just like Brooklyn to get the party started."

"Aye, I think your brothers are here somewhere. I saw Ronan flirting with the girls."

"I snort. He better watch it. His wife RSVPed."

"Really?" Joe looks at me surprised.

"Aye, not sure what made her want to come to this wedding, but she said she is. My baby brother might be in the bottle for the weekend."

He gives my waist a squeeze. "Dinna fash yerself."

I purr. "Oh, Scottish Joe is feeling at home. I love Scottish Joe."

He throws his head back with his laughs. "I remember you wanted nothing to do with my Scot ass."

I wink at him. "Ya grew on me. Changed me world, ye did."

Joe laughs louder as I prove how he rubbed off on me as I trade back and forth between our dialects. Our summers here over the years haven't helped.

I wouldn't have it any other way.

CHAPTER TWENTY-THREE

All Here

Ryan

I'm nervous all over again. This all needs to be perfect. The rehearsal went well, but we still have the dinner and speeches.

Carmen hasn't stopped smiling. I keep telling myself that's a good thing. Wyatt comes over and hands me Jordan. I can tell from the way Riley is peeking around Brax, these two just did something they shouldn't have.

I groan. This little girl is a troublemaker. I can no longer deny it.

"Ow, daddy," she says and pouts while holding her little hand to her chest.

Wyatt frowns. "Ow, my butt. The cat wouldn't have scratched you if you and Riley weren't trying to flush him."

"What's with you two trying to flush pets?" I ask.

Jordan shrugs, holding her hands up. She looks at me innocently. "They need church baths like Pop-pop Porter gives."

"That's it, Kaye. No more taking the kids to church with you when you babysit. They're going to catch a case and a line of sins hanging with you," I say.

"Little heathens need the Lord," my mother mutters as she comes to get Jordan to look after her hand.

I go to reply but my father is handed a mic right at that moment. He clears his throat as he stands from his seat.

I reach for Carmen's hand and give it a little squeeze. She looks at me with such happiness in her eyes. I lean in and kiss her lips. She squeezes my hand back.

"Thank you, Ry, this is all amazing."

Joe

"Well, we made it. Ryan drove us all crazy for almost a year and we are finally here. I'm proud of you, Ry. When he changed the location for the millionth time, I asked him why Scotland, why not get married in Ireland like his brothers. His words were 'It's where it began. You and mom married at the Black Castle. Since I'm the last, it should end there too. At least until the next generation.'

"I don't think my father could have been more proud of you boys. He would have loved to have you all here. Know it or not, every one of you have been connected by my Da. He planted the seeds for what would one day be the foundation of the Alliance. The man was a Grandmaster of chess and moved us all around the board to become who we are.

"I've watched kings born." I look to Logan, LaSalle, Uri, and Misha. "I've seen Queens made." My gaze falls on their wives. I place a fist over my chest and look to Roni, my Australian nephews, and my boys. "I've stood by as Knights were named and I've proudly watched you move the pawns as needed to get to the top. I, myself have played a pawn," I say as I place a hand on my wife's shoulder as she returns with Jordan in her arms.

"I couldn't see it in the beginning when my father sent me to Ireland to meet a young lass's father. This was his plan all along. Logan sat at my father's feet as he groomed him for what he and an old friend had planned before any of these lads were born.

"My father moved us around the globe as he saw fit, waiting for all the pieces to float together at a time such as this. I can connect the dots now as I watch his vision right before my eyes."

I smile and continue. "You will succeed in all you do because it was destined. It's in your blood to do great things. That goes for all you young lads. As for you Ryan. I know the best has yet to come. Don't see this as an end, son. This is the beginning of great joy and a new level of life and love."

I hand the mic over to Cass. She stands and smiles at Ry before turning to the crowd. I take my seat and get ready for whatever's about to come from her mouth.

"Phew. I didn't have to kill ye. I was sure I was going to have to choke the little fucker before we got to this day."

I chuckle. It wouldn't be Cassie if she didn't say what's on her mind. Everyone laughs as I look around. I'm grateful to my father for all he's done for us. I can't be the slightest mad for the mission he sent me on thirty-five years ago.

Cass continues. "I'm so happy for ye, me wee babe. The tallest of them all but still my wee one." She gets choked up and everyone starts to coo and clap.

"Carmen, I couldn't have asked for a better choice for his crazy, spoiled ass. Good luck to ye. Know this about the man you have married and will marry again.

"Ye will always come first, he will protect ye and make sure ye are loved. He will love ye children fiercely and make sure they want for nothing. I can promise ye this because this is the man we raised. The man I raised to be just like his father. I love ye, Ryan. I'm proud of ye, ye little shit."

Everyone roars with laughter. Another mic in the crowd comes to life, I look down the table to see Nicholas Lincoln has stood.

"Ryan." He pauses to purse his lips. "I'm glad you now have your own wife and child of your own so you can leave mine alone."

More laughter fills the room.

"We know they all still belong to me," Ry booms down the table and tosses Nick a wink.

"Cass, I'm not sure he's going to make it to tomorrow," Nick teases. "You get on my last nerve, but I'm happy for you, Black. Although, I didn't miss your wife has very similar mannerisms to mine."

"That's because you want to be just like me. For now, let's just say you have good taste," Ry taunts.

The laughs continue as speech after speech is given to rib Ryan and congratulate the happy couple. Again, my heart swells for my past and my future. A part of me wishes I could have talked Cass into one more try after Ryan was born.

CHAPTER TWENTY-FOUR

Almost There

Cassie

I fight to hold the tears back as Carmen stands before the mirror. Paloma did an amazing job designing and commissioning this gown. It speaks of Carmen and her Japanese heritage. She's going to take Ry's breath away in this dress.

The kimono style sleeves are stunning. The entire dress is made of sheer champagne colored, crystal covered fabric. The body of the dress falls in a mermaid style, outlining her curves perfectly.

Intricate patterns make the gown sparkle against Carmen's glowing skin. The crystals part down the center of her breasts in a deep V, giving the illusion of bare skin beneath all the crystals. A silk sash wraps her middle and ties in a bow at the back, creating a cathedral length train.

Jordan walks over to Carmen and leans against her mother's leg as she looks up at her, wearing an identical version of the kimono style dress sans sheer fabric. Her little dress is a champagne-colored silk.

"Pretty," Jordan says with a smile, showing her tiny little teeth.

"You like?" Carmen looks down at her and runs a hand over her curls.

Jordan nods. Carmen's face lights up as she spins to look at her mother and clasps her hands together in front of her chest.

"Mommy, this dress is everything," Carmen says through her emotions.

"Don't start dem tears," Paloma sings. "We can't keep fixing your face."

"I know, it's not me, it's the baby," she sniffles.

"You got lucky with the dress. Your butt gets wide with dem babies. Come let me put this comb in your hair," Paloma says, holding out the crystal covered comb.

Carmen frowns and turns her butt to the mirror. I suppress a laugh. You have to know Paloma to know she means no harm. The other girls in the room laugh as they snap pictures and coo over the bride.

A knock comes at the door. I know who or at least what it is. I rush over to open it. If someone ruins this, I'll have to murder me own son.

I open the door and take the box from Brooklyn. He smiles and gives me a wink. I reach to pat his cheek.

"Thank ya, love."

"No problem, Aunt Cass. Will ya be needing anything else?"

"No, I think we're good for now."

He nods and turns to leave. I close the door and move over to where Carmen sits with Jordan in her lap as Paloma places the comb in her large curls. It sits on her head like a crown, finishing the look almost perfectly.

However, it's the gift in this box that will absolutely finish the job. I hand Carmen the gift and take Jordan from her. Carmen opens the box and gasps as the diamond necklace comes into view. The lad did well. The necklace is gorgeous, it might just be more expensive than the one John gifted Roni. I pull it from the box to help her put it on.

The clusters of marquise shaped diamonds rest on her neck making her look like true royalty. I reach to wipe the tears from my eyes.

I look around the room. "How did me boys get so lucky. You are all so beautiful inside and out. You each love them in ways I could only dream to ask for. I never have to worry about who's taking care of me boys because I know they're safe in your arms. Now, keep the fuckers from eating me out of house and home and I'll be grateful to ye for life."

They all laugh. "I couldn't have asked for a better family," Nellie says.

"I've wanted to be a Black since I was a little girl. I haven't been disappointed," Bean says.

"Oh my God, Kaye," Roni groans. "If you don't put that pen down. I'm starting to hate talking around you. I never know what I might say that will end up in a book."

"I can't help it," Kaye whines, causing us all to laugh.

The laughter is interrupted by another knock at the door. I look at my watch. We still have some time before the ceremony is to start. I frown and move for the door.

When I open it, I'm floored. My brother's wife stands on the other side. A lot has changed about her since the last time I saw her. She's more stunning than the last time she graced us with her presence.

For one, her dreads are gone. They were gorgeous and healthy looking, but this suits her face. She's cut them off and now has a short curly afro of sorts as if she placed something in it to define the short curls. It's bright red and styled with a low fade on the sides and lines cut into one side of her head.

It all makes her eyes and freckles stand out. Her deep whiskey brown complexion makes the gorgeous freckles on her face astonishing. She has the most beautiful complexion to begin with. The way the bronze, yellows, and browns play in her coloring give her a glow that's too die for. I don't think I've ever seen her with more than mascara and lashes on. Maybe some lips gloss. Her skin is that flawless.

Ronan's going to lose his shit. I want to rush from the room to find him and let him know she's here. However, I pause. It's clear these two need to talk.

My train of thought comes to a screeching halt as Kaye rushes by me to pull my brother's wife into her arms. It's then that I notice my brother standing frozen in the hall. He looks handsome in his gray suit, the blue tie brings out the blue in his eyes.

Ronan has always made our red hair look damn good. I'm proud of my little brother for looking so smart, especially today. He'll have his wife in his arms before this night is over. I promise you that. I know it as sure as I know that look on his face. It's a look I've come to know well from my husband.

It's the look of a man who burns for the woman he loves. That's the look of a man ready to walk through hell and back to make this woman his in every way. I don't know what happened between the two, but I know Ronan cares for her.

I tap her on the shoulder. "Doll, I think you have someone looking for ye."

She turns for the door and her gasp is audible as she takes my brother in. He opens his arms for her. She only hesitates for a moment before she rushes into them.

I close the door behind her because the kiss Ronan lays on her once she's in his arms isn't something we should watch. It's too intimate. I can feel the passion from across the hall.

Joe

This is it. My boys and nephews stand around Ryan as he waits at the alter for the wedding to start. We've been trying to calm his nerves. I grab the back of his head and pull him down to kiss his forehead. "You're a fine lad. You did well."

"Thanks, Dad," he says nervously.

"You did really good, kid," John says. "The trees were a nice touch. You brought a little of all our worlds together."

"Fuck all them trees. I can't wait for the roti," Brax says, rubbing his stomach. "Feed me."

"You are a little shop of horrors," Wyatt teases.

"Bite me."

I reach to slap Brax upside the head. He rubs the spot and looks back at me with a frown. "For once, act like your mother and I didn't raise you with wolves."

He shrugs. "Like I didn't see you in the kitchen smooth talking your way into those little beef patties and some fish cakes."

I laugh because I indeed did hustle up some food before heading out here. "If you listened to anything we taught you, you'd be just as smooth."

"*Ohh*," my boys and nephews call out as they laugh.

"Brax, you're not ready for Uncle Joe," Logan says.

"Whatever, hey anyone seen Uncle Ronan?"

"Last I saw him, he said he was going to talk to Aunt Cass for a wee bit," Carrick replies.

"Maybe he found Jamie and the whiskey," Graham mutters.

"Nah, Jamie's been on the phone. His focus is somewhere else."

Just then the music starts to play, cutting off all conversation. Ryan looks like he's coming out of his skin. I shake my head and head toward my seat as Cass appears, looking as lovely as ever in her gray dress. I reach for her hand and give it a gentle squeeze.

I've been through so much with this woman. As I stand here waiting for my daughter-in-law to get to my son, my mind goes back to when we stood in the exact same spot to say our vows.

I remember being nervous, Wyatt's cry piercing the air as my Da rocked him in his arms. I remember the look in Cass's eyes as she stopped before me, just like Carmen does in the here and now.

It seemed like it took forever for me to remember to breathe. The sun shined behind Cass, placing a halo around her head. In that moment, I felt content. I didn't know this is what the future would bring, but here we stand.

We made it. Wyatt, Noah, Johnathan, Felix, Toby, Braxton, and Ryan—all precious gifts this woman beside me gifted me with. Year after year, I've been blessed with priceless moments I'll never forget. All the good has outweighed the bad.

EPILOGUE

Happy New Year

Joe

I turn the corner with little Connor in my arms. He has to use the bathroom. He's potty trained, but he doesn't know his way around.

"Hurry, Papa, hurry," he whispers. I can feel him clenching his cheeks. I get the feeling this will be more of a cleanup than I was expecting.

"I should have let your Grand take you." I purse my lips and shake my head.

We reach a restroom and I go to turn the knob. I freeze as moans come from behind the door.

"Ya will stop pushing me away." I hear between grunts. "I love ya. Tell me you understand this is over. I'll never be without ya again."

"I understand, Ro, I'm done pushing you away."

"Good," he groans.

I look down at Connor who's frowning at me. I snap out of it and rush for another bathroom as Connor breaks wind.

"And this is why we stopped at Ry," I remind myself.

Blue Collection Character Tree

Legally Bound 1

Bobby Mairettie and Paige Kemble-Mairettie *father and mother of:*

*Peyton and James Mairettie (*twin boys*)

*Sydney Mairettie and Maria Lynn Mairettie (*twin girls*)

Legally Bound 2

Marcus Mairettie and Rita Briggs-Mairettie *father and mother of:*

*Daniel Mairettie

*Hannah Mairettie

Legally Bound 3

Nathaniel (Nate) Briggs and Pamela (Pam) Kemble-Briggs *father and mother of:*

*Tiffany and Tracey Briggs (*twin girls*)

*Nathaniel Briggs Jr.

Legally Bound 4

Jasper Briggs and Marie Mairettie-Briggs *father and mother of:*

*Clay Briggs

The Mairettie Family

Grandpa Marcello Mairettie and Grandma Marie Ann *father and mother of:*

*Marcello Mairettie Jr.

*Andrew Mairettie
*James Mairettie
*Jessie Mairettie
*Lynn Mairettie
*Gianna Mairettie
*James Mairettie and Minnie Mairettie *father and mother of:*
    *Bobby Mairettie
    *Sam Mairettie – (Ellen Kensington-Mairettie, *wife*)
    *Marcus Mairettie
    *Marie Mairettie

The Briggs Family

Thomas Briggs and Raquel Marinos-Briggs (***Deceased***) *father and mother of:*

*Nathaniel Briggs
*Rita Briggs

Earl Briggs (Thomas' younger brother) and Caitronia Marinos-Briggs (twin sister of Raquel) *father and mother of:*

*Kelly Briggs-Fecteau (Alexie Fecteau, *husband*)
*Jasper Briggs

The Kemble Family

Peyton Kemble and Davina Kemble *father and mother of:*

*Pamela Kemble
*Paige Kemble

Other Important *Legally Bound* Characters

Camille (Cam) Mc Wien-Carter (Seth Carter, *soon-to-be ex-husband*) *father and mother of:*

*Seth Carter Jr.

*Eddie Carter
*Aiden Carter

Austin Mc Wien (*Camille's father*)

Baroness Olivia Kontos (Baron Kontos' widow; Jasper's ex-lover; Thomas Briggs' new love interest)

Vanessa (Julissa) Smith-Mims (Patrick Mims, *husband,* ***Deceased***)

Hush 1

Uri Donati and Valentina Caprisi-Donati *father and mother of:*
*Vita Khayla Donati
*Nori Donati
*Inzo Donati
*Eva Donati

Hush 2

Luca Donati and Shannon Caprisi-Donati *father and mother of:*
*Carlo Donati (Introduced in **Ballers 2**)

The Donati Family

Angelo Uri Donati (***Deceased***) and Donatella Manzo-Donati-~~Zuko~~ *father and mother of:*
*Uri Donati
*Nico Donati ~~Zuko~~
*Annabella Donati ~~Zuko~~ (*Nico's twin sister*)
*Michael Donati – ~~Zuko~~

Nicholas Donati (Angelo Donati's brother) and Ava Donati *father and mother of:*

*Luca Donati

The Caprisi Family

Vincent Caprisi and Khayla Grant-Caprisi (***Deceased***) *father and mother of:*

*Valentina Caprisi
*Lissette Caprisi (***Deceased***)
**Shannon Caprisi (*Vincent's daughter*)

Other Important *Hush* Characters

Uncle Valentine Caprisi (*Vincent's brother; head hitter*)

Iman Grant (*Khayla's sister; **Shannon's mother;* ***Deceased***)

Roberto Donati-Zuko (*Donatella's husband;* ***Deceased***)
***Posed as Dale the accountant from Legally Bound 3*

Cole 'Brooklyn' O'Brien

DJ

Ballers 1

Bradley Monroe and Tamara Hathaway-Monroe *father and mother of:*

*Brielle Monroe
*Ashley Monroe and Ashton Monroe (*twins*)
*Corey Monroe (*Baby Tam is pregnant with at end of* ***Ballers 1***)

The Monroe Family

Vernon Monroe and Gloria Monroe *father and mother of:*

*Trevor Monroe (Donna, *soon to be ex-wife)*

*Bradley Monroe

*Ann Monroe (*Bradley's twin sister; Tom, husband*)

Trevor Monroe and Donna Monroe *father and mother of:*

*Jessica Monroe

*Toby Monroe and Paige Monroe (*twins*)

*Jonathan Monroe

Tom Rivers and Ann Monroe-Rivers *father and mother of:*

*George Rivers and Melissa Rivers (*twins*)

*Amy Rivers

The Hathaway Family

Byron Hathaway and Fiona Hathaway *father and mother of:*

*Ellerie Hathaway

*Tamara Hathaway

Other Important *Ballers* Characters

Stacey (Tam's best friend)

Reese (Tam's best friend; Nico's girlfriend in ***Ballers 1***)

Alee (Tam's best friend)

Cyrus Pierson (Tam's boss) *father of:*

*Tommy Pierson

*Carey Pierson

*Stephanie Pierson

Ballers 2

Nico Donati and Reese Bridges-Donati *father and mother of:*

*Nico Donati Jr.

*Lanya Donati

*Orso Donati

*Santo Donati

*Stefano Donati

Other Important *Ballers 2* **Characters**

Tiberius Roman (Reese's ex-husband)

Symphony (Michael's right-hand)

Brothers Black 1

Wyatt Black and Lanelle (Nellie) Bryant-Black *father and mother of:*

*Nora Black

*Evan Black

The Black Family

Joseph Black and Cassidy Black *father and mother of:*

*Wyatt Black

*Noah Black

*Johnathan Black

*Felix Black

*Toby Black

*Braxton Black

*Ryan Black

The Lockhart Family

Rob Lockhart and Faith Lockhart *father and step-mother of:*

*Heather Lockhart

Steve Lockhart and Nora Bryant-Lockhart (***Deceased***) *step-father and mother of:*

*Lanelle (Nellie) Bryant-Black

Chase Lockhart and Jennifer Lockhart *father and mother of:*

*Rebecca (Bean) Lockhart (Noah's best friend and love interest)

Other Important *Brothers Black 1* **Characters**

Missy (Johnathan's ex-girlfriend, ***Deceased***)

Lucy (*Heather's girlfriend*)

Barry Coleman (***Deceased***)

Brothers Black 2

Noah Black and Rebecca (Bean) Lockhart-Black *father and mother of:*

*Brodie Black

*Connor Black

**Baby unnamed*

Other Important *Brothers Black 2* Characters

Joshua (***Deceased***)

Carmen (Nene) Nash (*reporter; niece of Mariah Briggs from Yours Series; Ryan's new crush*)

Logan O'Brien

Brothers Black 3

King Toby Black and Queen Ogeima Feechi (Kamara) Abioye-*Black father and mother of:*

  *Lulu Black

  *TJ Black

  **Baby on the way*

Other Important *Brothers Black 3* **Characters**

Missy (Johnathan's ex-girlfriend, ***Deceased***)

Lucy (*Heather's girlfriend*)

Barry Coleman (***Deceased***)

King Elijah Abioye aka Mr. Naidoo

Queen Ada Catherine Naidoo-Abioye

King Kwäzē Naidoo-Abioye

Celeste (Kwäzē's ex-girlfriend)

King Afafa (***Deceased***)

Missy (Johnathan's ex-girlfriend, ***Deceased***)

Lucy (*Heather's girlfriend*)

Barry Coleman (***Deceased***)

Joshua (***Deceased***)

Carmen Nash aka Nene (*Reporter, Mariah Briggs, from Yours Series, Niece, Ryan's new crush*)
Logan O'Brien

Dylan O'Brien

Jamie O'Brien

Cole 'Brooklyn' O'Brien

Uncle Jonah McGowan

Uncle Jack McGowan

Uncle Raymond McGowan

Uncle Ronan McGowan

Carrick McGowan

Malcolm McGowan

Graham McGowan

Jeremiah McGowan

Reilly McGowan

Brothers Black 4

Braxton Black and Heather Lockhart-Black *father and mother of:*

*Riley Black

*Rowen Black

Other Important ***Brothers Black 4*** **Characters**

Debbie ~~Lockhart~~-Kline (Rob's ex-wife, Heather's Mother)

Lucy (*Heather's pretend girlfriend*)

Amanda Kline (Heather's half-sister)

Ernest Kline (Heather's Stepfather, ***Deceased***)

Eugene aka Crooked Nose

Logan O'Brien

Dylan O'Brien

Jamie O'Brien

Cole 'Brooklyn' O'Brien

Uncle Jonah McGowan

Uncle Jack McGowan

Uncle Raymond McGowan

Uncle Ronan McGowan

Carrick McGowan

Malcolm McGowan

Graham McGowan

Jeremiah McGowan

Reilly McGowan

Nicholas Lincoln

Sephora Lincoln

Thomas Briggs

Brothers Black 5

Felix Black and Kaye Porter-Black aka Kaye Blaze *father and mother of:*

*Dashawn Black

*Second child unannounced

Other Important ***Brothers Black 5*** **Characters**

Lakia Redding (*Kaye's writer friend*)

Dean (*Kaye's writer friend*)

Hayidah (*Doll for Club Desire*)

Pastor Wayne Porter (*Kaye's father*)

Danesha Porter (*Kaye's mother*)

Danny Porter (***Deceased*** *Kaye's brother and Felix's best friend*)

Grandma Reid (*Kaye's grandmother*)

Grandpa Reid (*Kaye's grandfather*)

Alberto Perez (*Felix's best friend*)

Jacob McTavish (*Lead actor in Kaye's movie*)

Mona Richards (***Deceased****, a fan)*

Logan O'Brien

Dylan O'Brien

Jamie O'Brien

Cole 'Brooklyn' O'Brien

Connie O'Brien

Kate O'Brien

Uncle Ronan McGowan

Carrick McGowan

Brothers Black 6

Ryan Black and Carmen Nash *father and mother of:*

*Jordan Black

*Second child unborn

Other Important *Brothers Black 6* **Characters**

Kiyoshi Matsumara-Nash (*Carmen's father*)

Paloma Matsumara-Nash (*Carmen's mother*)

Nelson "Ne" Matsumara-Nash (*Carmen's Brother*)

Yui (*Nelson assistant*)

Bekia

Calu

Mariah Briggs (*Carmen's Aunt*)

Gigi (*Carmen's roommate*)

Torque

Alexander (*Oldest Triplet*)

Maximilian aka Mil (*Middle Triplet*)

Tobias (*Youngest Triplet*)

Austin Mc Wien (***Now Deceased***)

Logan O'Brien

Misha Krupin

Dr. Omid V-Shah

Connie O'Brien

Kate O'Brien

Don LaSalle Locatelli

Tasha Locatelli

Valentine Donati

Uri Donati

Brothers Black 7

Johnathan Black and Cherone "Roni" Pérez -Black *father and mother of:*

*Mena Black

Other Important *Brothers Black 7* **Characters**

Natasha "Indigo"

Grissel Pérez (**Now Deceased**)

Eliam Pérez (**Now Deceased**)

Irina Krupin (**Now Deceased**)

Yours Series

Nicholas Lincoln and Sephora (Sophi/Soph/Lilla du) Emilsson *father and mother of:*

*Nicole Lincoln
*Nadia Lincoln
*Nicholas Lincoln Jr.

The Lincoln Family

Dean Lincoln and Shelly Lincoln (***Both Deceased***) *father and mother of:*

*Nicholas Lincoln
*Rick ~~Carbon~~ Lincoln
*Gavin ~~Carbon~~ Lincoln

The Emilsson Family

Liam Emilsson (thought to be deceased) and Faraz Emilsson father and mother of:

*Lucian Emilsson
*Ettie Emilsson
*Sephora Emilsson

Lucian Emilsson and Kimberly Ann Clove *father and mother of:*

*Lilla Emilsson

Other Important *Yours* Characters

Mark Fienberg (Sephora's best friend)

Ivana Graves (Nick's ex-girlfriend; ***Deceased***)

Bianca (Liam's mistress; ***Missing***)

Winston (Nick's driver and security)

Jillian Carver (Nick's ex-temporary PA; ***Deceased***)

Harvey Carver (Jillian's father; Nick's family friend; ***Deceased***)

Bailey Wilder (waitress; Mark's girlfriend)

Dylan O'Brien

Nick's Crew
Wyatt Black
Kevin Briggs (Mariah Briggs' husband; Nick's PA)
Craig Hilton
George Ligal
Lucian Emilsson
Andrew Connor (Ettie's husband)

Be Yours Series
Prince Omid Arman Vahid (Dr. O.V-Shah) and Divine Favors
father and mother of:
*Prince Firuz Arman Vahid
*Princess Fairuza Araz Vahid

The Vahid Family

Javed Vahid and Hana Vahid (**third wife**) *father and mother of:*

*Prince Omid Arman Vahid

*Prince Bazar Vahid

Padma Vahid *first wife and mother of:*

*Prince Paiman Vahid

*Princess Yasmin Vahid

Other Important *Be Yours* Characters

Prince Jahan Vahid

Prince Remi Vahid

Prince Ramses Vahid

Sassa Vahid (*First wife of Javed Vahid*)

Marica Thompson (Divine's cousin)

Dr. Nobi

Gretta (Medical Assistant)

Navid (Omid's advisor)

Dada (Divine's best friend)

ACKNOWLEDGMENTS

Thank you, Lord. This book is done. The agony. I wanted to get them right and tell the right story. I've told exactly what they showed me they needed me to tell. It was fun to have this final visit into the Black world.

It's so long to the Black but not goodbye. We will see them again. I need to read through so much to close these worlds but I'm excited about it.

Thank you to all of my readers for following me and my many worlds and for allowing me to be the author and tell the stories of my heart's desire. It's so much fun to get to create and find the story the characters want to tell. It can also be taxing, so thank you for understanding each book needs time. As always, thank you for every email, message, and post. Love you guys to life!

Thank you to my husband. His wisdom is so in season. He keeps pushing me when I'm ready to give up. Thanks, Boo.

I'm going to stand up and give God praise! To God be the glory. I've been pressing through and He keeps blessing. I'm going to say His name because He's making sure the world says mine. And even if that weren't so. He deserves all the glory. New blessings for team Blue. Thank you, Lord.

Next! Kelex comes to a close. Back to work.

ABOUT THE AUTHOR

Blue Saffire, award-winning, bestselling author of over thirty contemporary romance novels and novellas, writes with the intention to touch the heart and the mind. Blue hooks, weaves, and loops multiple series, keeping you engaged in her worlds. Blue is a hybrid author, writing for her own publishing company Perceptive Illusions as Blue Saffire as well as Royal Blue.

Blue and her husband live in a house filled with laughter and creativity, in Long Island, NY. Both working hard to build the Blue brand and cultivate their love for the artists. Creative is their family affair.

Blue holds an MBA in Marketing and Project Management, as well as a MED in Instructional Technology and Curriculum Design. She is also an NLP Master Practitioner.

Wait, there is more to come! You can stay updated with my latest releases, learn more about me, the author, and be a part of contests by subscribing to my newsletter at
www.BlueSaffire.com
If you enjoyed A Black Christmas, I'd love to hear your thoughts and please feel free to leave a review. And when you do, please let me know by emailing me TheBlueSaffire@gmail.com or leave a comment on Facebook https://www.facebook.com/BlueSaffireDiaries or Twitter @TheBlueSaffire

Other books by Blue Saffire

Placed in Best Reading Order

Also available....

Legally Bound

Legally Bound 2: Against the Law

Legally Bound 3: His Law

Perfect for Me

Hush 1: Family Secrets

Ballers: His Game

Brothers Black 1: Wyatt the Heartbreaker

Legally Bound 4: Allegations of Love

Hush 2: Slow Burn

Legally Bound 5.0: Sam

Yours 1: Losing My Innocence

Yours 2: Experience Gained

Yours 3: Life Mastered

Ballers 2: His Final Play

Legally Bound 5.1: Tasha Illegal Dealings

Brothers Black 2: Noah

Legally Bound 5.2: Camille

Legally Bound 5.3 & 5.4 Special Edition

Where the Pieces Fall

Legally Bound 5.5: Legally Unbound

Brothers Black 4: Braxton the Charmer

My Funny Valentine

Broken Soldier

Remember Me

Brothers Black 5: Felix the Watcher

A Home for Christmas

Be My Valentine

Coming Soon...

Lost Souls Book 4: Again

*The A**hole Club Book 6: Kelex*

The Lost Souls MC Series

Forever

Never

Always

The A Million to Blow Series

A Million to Blow

A Million to Stay

A Million Blown Coming soon...

Blue Saffire Exclusive on the

BlueSaffire.com Site

His Miracle Baby

Razor

Other books from Evei Lattimore Collection

Books by Blue Saffire

Black Bella 1

Destiny 1: Life Decisions

Destiny 2: Decisions of the Next Generation

Destiny 3 coming soon...

Star

Other books from Royal Blue Gay Romance

Collection written by Blue Saffire

Kyle's Reveal

Beau's Redemption

Lost Souls Series
Forever
Never
lways
BLUE SAFFIRE
Forever: Book 1-Brick
Never: Book 2 -Gutter
Always: Books 3-King
Again: Book 4-Cage
Before 4.5- Thor
Sometimes: Book 5-Jackie
Lifetime: Book 6-Grim
Still: Book 7-Kevlar
Once: Book 8-Diggs, Axle, and Sugar
Now: Book 9 -Tracks
When: Book 10-Holden
BLUESAFFIRE.COM

www.ingramcontent.com/pod-product-compliance
Lightning Source LLC
Chambersburg PA
CBHW061543250926
52052CB00010B/3044
9781941924129